AF424342

Avoiding Love

AN ENEMIES-TO-LOVERS SECRET-BABY ROMANCE

BETTY RUDER

© Copyright 2022 - All rights reserved.

It is not legal to reproduce, duplicate, or transmit any part of this document in either electronic means or in printed format. Recording of this publication is strictly prohibited and any storage of this document is not allowed unless with written permission from the publisher except for the use of brief quotations in a book review.

This book is a work of fiction. Any resemblance to persons, living or dead, or places, events or locations is purely coincidental.

Prologue

NATALIA

The sound of a baby crying woke me, and I bolted upright in bed to look around. *Why had I heard a baby?* No one in my apartment complex had a child. It was an adult-only building, and I rented it purposely so I didn't have to listen to the sounds of children.

I listened for a while, but the sound did not come again. I curled back up and pulled the blanket over my head. I had to be up for work shortly, and I wanted to sleep every second I could.

I was dozing back off when my stomach suddenly heaved. Vomit filled my mouth, and I unwound myself from the confines of my blanket and ran for the bathroom. But I was too late. Last night's meal dripped down the front of my pajamas.

Great, I thought. *I must have caught a stomach bug.*

Hopping into the shower, I washed away the contents of my stomach. Then my belly lurched again, but there was nothing but bile this time.

I couldn't even remember the last time I'd been sick. It had me concerned.

I broke out the thermometer, but my temperature was average. I figured it would probably get better if I were up and about, so I got dressed and did my makeup for work. When I put on my favorite pair of slacks, I was shocked to find they didn't fit. I blamed the stomach ache and bloating and found pants with a more relaxed waist.

There was no way I was going to miss a day. The job meant too much to me. I had beat out hundreds of candidates for an entry-level position with Prism Media, and I had never taken a day off. My goal was to be on the company's board of directors within five years, and I wouldn't get that position without hard work and dedication. Missing a day was not an option.

As I sat at my kitchen table with a piece of dry toast, I began to feel sick again. When I got to the bathroom, I hugged the toilet, and up came the toast. This was getting ridiculous.

I called my cousin Rory for advice. I told him about the vomiting and that my pants didn't fit.

"Sounds like you're pregnant," he said calmly. "You looked like you put on weight the last time I saw you. I would get a pregnancy test."

I explained that I was too sick to go far, and he offered to pick up a pregnancy kit for me. I was highly skeptical that I was pregnant. The last time I'd had sex had been at least four months ago, and it had been a one-night stand.

When trying to remember the last time I'd had a period, I realized I couldn't say when that was. Fear gripped me. I wasn't ready for a baby at my age. I had a promising career and big plans for my future. A baby had never even come to mind, and I was too career driven to consider having a child. Plus, I wasn't even sure I liked children.

A knock came at my door, and I let Rory in. He had bought three kits, unsure of which to use. I grabbed one randomly and went to urinate on the stick. I sat there, afraid of the results. I set the pregnancy stick on the counter so I didn't watch the plus or negative sign when it appeared. After a few minutes, I looked at it, and it was positive

This time when I vomited, it had nothing to do with morning sickness.

"Give me another test," I ordered Rory, and he dutifully passed me another one.

I repeated the process, but this time, two pink lines showed up. My chest felt tight, and I began hyperventilating. Two tests couldn't give me false positives, but I asked Rory for the last pregnancy test.

Without a word and with a solemn face, he handed me the last test. "They were both positive, weren't they?"

I slammed the door in his face, not daring to speak.

When I looked at the final test, it, too, showed that I was pregnant.

Collapsing on the floor, I began to weep. I heard Rory jiggle the lock and tell me to open the door. But I couldn't. My whole life had changed in a matter of minutes. *How could anyone understand what I was going through?* I wanted to be a career woman, not a mother. I was only twenty-one, for fuck's sake.

The door jiggled again, but this time, it swung open. Rory looked at the three positive tests and squatted down to hug me. "We'll get through this together, no matter what happens." He calmly stroked my hair. "Who's the father?" he asked, his curiosity piqued.

"It has to be Cassius Baxter, from three or four months back. We hooked up at a conference."

Rory let out an appreciative whistle. "Well, at least you don't have to worry about child support. He's got loads of money."

"It's not about money, Rory. I don't know if I want to keep the baby."

He suddenly had a frown on his face. "Of course, you have to keep it. It's your child, and I know you wouldn't be the same if you did away with it."

All I could do was weep. Rory was right. It didn't matter who the father was. I knew I would keep the child. But I would never let Cassius Baxter know.

Regretfully, I called into work sick, and Rory tucked me back into bed with a bucket.

"We are in this together," he said. "I will help you with anything you need. You know that."

"I do," I mumbled before my tears started to fall.

This was my baby, and there was no way I would share it with a money-hungry business tycoon like Cassius. I wanted this child to have a good upbringing the way my mother raised me. Screw Cassius Baxter. This baby would be all mine, no matter what I had to do. Feeling suddenly protective of the tiny life inside me, I rested my hand on my abdomen, wondering if it was a boy or girl.

Chapter One

NATALIA

Three and a half months ago...

If I knew one thing, it was how to read people. And this smooth-talking gentleman was doing his best to get me into bed with him. It wasn't the first time this had happened over the week-long conference. It seemed like every man, married or single, took advantage of conferences to leave their regular life and wife behind so they could hook up with another person.

I could see it in the reverse tan line circles around the men's fingers. This one still had the indentation of his ring on his left ring finger. He was trying to cover it up, but he talked animatedly with his hands and often unintentionally revealed it.

I nodded at what I thought were appropriate times, not really listening to what he said. The man looked dumpy, even in a full three-piece suit. The tufts coming out of his ears were almost as thick as the hair coming out of his nose. He really needed to invest in a trimmer.

"Your hair looks as soft as cornsilk," he said, leaning in as if to kiss me.

I leaned away and made an excuse to leave the conversation. "I'm sorry," I said, "I need to get a bite to eat and rest. Enjoy the rest of the conference, and travel home safely to your wife and kids."

His eyes bulged out of his head, and his cheeks puffed, but I had briskly walked away before I had to listen to his lies about not having a family.

As I said, I was just good at reading people. It was what had made me enter the marketing industry.

I walked to the pub and sat in a booth, secretly hoping no one would approach me. A cute waitress with short blond hair came and dropped off a glass of water before asking if I was ready to order. Though I was ravenous with hunger, I hadn't yet looked at the menu to know what I would eat. Maybe a burger or some chicken wings.

That probably wasn't what I should be eating, considering I was watching my waistline. But then again, I planned on catching a good buzz before drifting off to sleep tonight, and I didn't want to have a few drinks on an empty stomach.

Once I went home, I would officially be starting my first day as an entry-level marketer for Prism Media. This conference was the kickoff to what I hoped to be a long and lustrous career. I couldn't wait to get back and get my new office laid out, and I had already bought an aloe plant for my desk.

There would also be a photograph of my late parents, but I didn't want to think of that depressing topic now.

The pub was starting to fill up, and I felt pretty inconspicuous using a whole booth to myself. Then a man with curly blond hair slid into the seat across from me. His arms were muscularly beefy, and he had a square jaw that I could probably smash rocks on.

When seated, he turned to me and asked, "Do you mind if I sit here, darling?"

I thought about it for a moment, then gestured to where he already sat. "I don't think I have much of an option."

"Well, that's not true," he said.

He slurred his words a bit, but was it an accent or from drink?

"You always have an option," he said. "Seriously, feel free to kick me out."

I eyed him speculatively, deciding he was a few sheets to the wind and it wouldn't hurt to sit and talk to the man. I subtly checked his ring finger and saw no tan lines or impressions. So he was single or had a girlfriend, and I wouldn't know which until he gave it away somehow.

"You have beautiful eyes, princess." The term of endearment and compliment felt special for some reason. I doubted he was as bold with other women. Then again, since he had the body of a god and a killer smile, I figured he got along with ladies quite well.

He turned that smile on me, and I felt a tremble in my core. His eyes held me captive in his gaze like a mouse by a snake's charm. I wanted this man, and I was pretty sure sitting with me had been an intentional move on his part instead of having to do with seating issues in the busy pub.

"Let me buy you a drink," he said, signaling the waitress with a twenty in his hand.

He handed her the money and ordered two rum and colas. I was impressed when he didn't even look at her ass as she walked away. Even I couldn't help but look. He also gave her a significant tip, which impressed me.

Men who didn't tip and wore brand-new Rolexes on their wrists were ignorant louts. At least this man had class. I could tell he was wealthy by the cut of his clothes. They were fitted for his form perfectly, showing off his broad shoulders and tapered waist. His shoes were buffed and polished, and his tie had been loosened as if to signify he was officially off company time.

"Cassius Baxter," he said, holding out his hand to shake mine.

"I'm Natalia," I said.

I had heard that name before. He was a very wealthy business tycoon, who owned companies all over the world, and he was way out of my league.

"Pleased to meet you, madame." He kissed the back of my hand delicately, then released it as the waitress arrived with our drinks.

Cassius threw his drink back and ordered another one immediately. It appeared as if this business tycoon was a bit of a lush.

We ordered chicken wings and nachos and decided to share them between the two of us. Chicken wings were my life, and I dug into them like a pig snorting for truffles. I noticed him continually looking at me as I ate, making me a bit self-conscious. But I was ravenously hungry, and I figured I would never see the guy again, so there was no reason to make it a big deal.

"Watching you eat is so sensual," he said, leaning across the table to wipe some dipping sauce from the corner of my mouth.

The touch of his hand was so warm it almost burned me, and I felt the heat of his gaze as he inspected what I had in my shirt.

Soon the food had disappeared from the plates, and the waitress came around to offer us dessert and drinks. I declined, but he ordered another drink.

I decided then that it was time for me to leave. I stuck out my hand for a shake. Once again, Cassius's lips lingered over the back of my long, gel-lacquer nails.

"It was a pleasure to dine with you. Take my card. If you want to reach me, it has my personal number on it."

I fingered the beautifully embossed card and knew I would be throwing it into the trash the first chance I got. A man like that would only want one thing from me. He was wealthy and connected, and I was just starting an entry-level position.

Our worlds did not flow together, but I thanked him and left some money on the table for the server.

When I got to my hotel room, I fell onto the bed and let loose a sigh. That man had been so sexy. I wish I were bold enough to consider a one-night stand. But that was not my way. I was a poised professional and did not give in to encounters like those.

I slipped into a white camisole and matching lace booty shorts. When washing my face, I thought I heard a knock on the door.

It stopped, and I paused to see if another knock would fall on the wood of the door, but whoever it was left. I crawled into bed and pulled the soft covers over my body. It didn't take me long to fall asleep, but shortly after, someone started knocking on the door again, waking me from a dream where Cassius was kissing other parts of my body besides the back of my hand.

"I'm coming!" I called out.

When I opened the door, in strolled Cassius. I pinched myself, thinking that this was still a part of my dream, but the pain was real enough.

"What are you doing here?" I asked, my interest piqued.

"I thought this was my room." He slurred. "This keycard doesn't work in this door."

"That's because it's my room. Do you want me to help you find your room?"

"No, I'll just stay here if that's all right with you. You're gorgeous, and I can think of a hundred things I want to do to you right now."

Feeling abnormally bold, I said, "Then do them."

I almost jumped back as he suddenly reached for me, pulling me into his arms. He lifted me up, then his firm lips pressed against mine, and our tongues mingled as we deepened the kiss. His arms felt even more prominent than in my dreams, and I could see and feel the bulge under his suit.

His hands went to the lace spaghetti straps of my camisole, and he slipped my top off in a smooth motion. For a man that was three sheets to the wind, he was surprisingly agile and gentle.

I reached down to his hard cock and stroked it through the fabric. He took his belt off for me and placed my hand on his zipper. I slowly lowered it as if to tease him.

He groaned. "You are so fucking hot."

When I released his thick and veiny penis from the confines of his pants, he let loose a satisfied sigh.

Not believing what I was about to do with a stranger, I had a moment of discomfort. As if reading my body language, he began kissing the tops of my C-cup-sized breasts. He squeezed them gently with his large hands and rubbed the bud of my nipples with his palms. Warmth spread through them and into my belly.

He then rubbed the outside of my underwear with a finger as he left a trail of light pecks from my breasts down my stomach to the edge of my panties. Instead of moving the underwear covering my pussy, he began to lick and nuzzle my clit through the lacy fabric. It felt sensational. No one had ever done it to me before.

He picked me up effortlessly and laid me down on the bed. I hadn't realized how tall he was until I was in his arms. I lay back and spread my legs.

He moved the fabric of my panties to the side with a finger and delved deep with his tongue. He slipped two fingers inside of me and found my G-spot quickly. He altered the pace and pressure of his fingers, and soon my panties were wet. His tongue constantly changed patterns, keeping me quivering and curling my toes.

Soon I felt my pussy start to contract, and the sheets beneath us were suddenly sodden. I had never squirted before in my life, and I began to sit up and apologize profusely.

He crawled up beside me and brushed my long chocolate-brown hair out of my face. "It was marvelous and turned me on so much that I have to fuck you right now."

He rolled on top of me and slid his penis in effortlessly. I was dripping wet now, and he whispered, "You feel so good." His voice was raspy with desire.

Cassius's cock had significant girth and length. Having him inside me as his muscular body lay atop was one of the best moments in my sexual history. It just felt right, like we were destined for this one night of bliss. He did not ram me, but instead, he rocked gently and slowly in and out of me.

Soon, I felt my temperature rise and my heartbeat increase. I was going to orgasm again, and the sexy grunts that fell from Cassius's lips increased my lust for this fine specimen of a man. We both let loose cries to the heavens when we came together.

He lay on top of me for a long while. I liked how he made me feel like I was worth protecting as he sheltered me with his body.

"I'm sorry," he apologized, "I didn't mean to crush you. Are you all right?"

"I am more than all right," I said.

He gave me a cocky grin. "I thought you'd say that, judging by the way I made you squeal."

"I do not squeal during sex," I claimed. "I'm not a pig."

"You're right. You are not a pig. You just sound like one."

I swatted his arm playfully as he laughed loudly. Its deep booming sound made me want to laugh with him.

"I have to sleep," he said.

I looked at the time and realized my flight was in two hours. I had to get out of here quickly.

"Okay, I'll be right back," I said, heading to the bathroom to clean up, but when I returned, Cassius was snoring softly, his arms wrapped around his pillow.

Knowing that this encounter would never lead to more than a one-night stand, I set his card on the end table. We lived in two separate worlds, and I would never fit in his perfect life. I was nothing but a poor girl with few prospects. When he woke from his drunken stupor, he would see it and reject me. It was better this way.

That was that, I said to myself. I collected my belongings and headed out of the hotel and into the red light of dawn.

Chapter Two

CASSIUS

Five years later...

I tapped my foot impatiently. The driver was supposed to be here five minutes ago, and I was still waiting. I debated firing the man, as this was the second time he was not where he was supposed to be. One thing I couldn't stand was tardiness. I was never late and held everyone to the same standards. If they couldn't meet my expectations, then they were dispensable. I didn't become a billionaire by accepting half-assed measures and excuses.

I had recently bought Prism Media, a marketing company that catered to high-class clientele. I'd searched for a good company that I could purchase so I did not have to rely on other businesses for my marketing needs. It was also a great deal, as the owner had passed away and the board of directors was a joke.

I planned to do away with the whole group and replace them with people I knew I could rely on. Though, I had faith in very few people in general. I had learned early in life that people were not to be trusted. My own father had stolen my first love away, and I had ruined the man and his business as repayment for that betrayal. It had left me bitter, but at least I accepted that aspect of myself.

Today was the first time I would visit the company. I expected that Prism Media would need a lot of micromanaging before it could function at its best, and I was ready to make the necessary staff cuts. I would have a whole host of new enemies before the day ended, but someone had to carry that burden. It was what a CEO was for. I had to make difficult and unpopular decisions, just like I always had.

My driver finally arrived, and I gave him a scorching look. "Late again," I said to the driver, who looked appropriately cowed.

"I won't let it happen again, boss," he mumbled.

"See that you don't, or you'll be driving a taxi again in no time." I slipped into the back of the car and grabbed a seltzer from the built-in fridge. I always seemed to be dealing with the incompetence of others. Sometimes, I wondered how I managed to get through the day without knocking someone's head in with my fist.

The drive was surprisingly short, and when I saw the building, my first thoughts were how I would need to reface the entire structure or buy a new one. I was surprised at how ugly the façade was, and it just wouldn't do. I began mentally making a list of things to do. I would also have to hire a local personal assistant. My current PA would not relocate due to family. I didn't understand that loyalty to family. But I knew that it was due, in large part, to being raised in a boarding school and not by loving parents.

The last I had heard from my mother were curses as I took her supply of prescription meds and flushed them down the toilet. I hadn't been allowed on the family estate since. But it didn't bother me much, and it wasn't really my home, anyway. I never bothered putting down roots, knowing that life was transient and nothing lasted. It was a pessimistic view, but it helped me keep my sanity.

I got out of the car and walked up the front stairs, my eyes taking in every detail. That was why I noticed the cleaning staff would need replacing and the receptionist required a proper, professional desk. We had to demonstrate prestige for the clientele I would be bringing to Prism Media. Judging by my first impression, it would be months before I could invite my colleagues. They would turn their noses up with one look at this excuse for an office.

When I entered through the glass doors, I saw no staff present. That struck me as odd. I checked my watch and saw that it was after nine, so someone should be around, but all the desks were still empty.

I had to investigate the reason why. Then, suddenly, I heard hollering and music coming from somewhere. I turned a corner following the noise and saw where the staff had gone. There were balloons and streamers, cake and presents. *Are they celebrating someone's birthday?* I wondered. Then I read the banner. "Congratulations on your promotion, Natalia," it read.

At the center of all the mirth was a familiar-looking woman with long hair past her slender waist and wide hips that I couldn't help but admire. She was dressed to the nines in a long velvety green dress and wore a party hat, ruining her put-together look. But that smile could strike a man dead, and I saw that many of the men and women in the room were admiring her.

I briefly wondered what position she now held and figured that I would most likely be firing her before she actually obtained the position. *It's too bad,* I thought. She was a stunner.

The woman seemed so familiar to me, but I couldn't quite place her. I racked my brain, but where I had seen her previously wouldn't come to me.

A woman bumped into me and turned to look. She clearly liked what she saw by the wide grin she gave me.

"Where is the CEO's office?" I asked curtly.

"I'm sorry, sir, but our CEO died a few weeks ago. We have yet to meet the new one, but the office is in the far right corner of this floor. You can't miss it." She grinned again. "Can I help you with anything?" She was insinuating more than just assistance in finding the office, which repelled me immediately.

"No." I waved her away and went in the direction she pointed. I would also have to redo my new office, judging by the building. I sighed and strode purposely past the revelers. No one seemed to pay me any attention, for which I was grateful. The last thing I wanted to do was fake interest in the celebration.

When I reached the corner office, I was pleasantly surprised. It was expansive with large mahogany doors and glass walls with fitted blinds. I jiggled the doorknob to find that somebody had locked it, and I almost punched the door in frustration. *Was anything going to go right today?*

No one was on this side of the building, and I doubted a random person would just happen to be carrying a spare set of keys. I would have to break up the celebration so I could get some work done today. I set down my laptop and briefcase in a nearby cubicle and headed toward the party.

I wondered why they didn't bother to wait until the end of the day to celebrate but figured it was an excuse for the employees to slack off. I grabbed the arm of a passing man and asked him who was in charge.

"You see the lady in the party hat? She's in charge until our new CEO gets here."

"That would be me," I said and watched as the man's brown eyes opened wide in shock.

"I am so sorry, Mr. Baxter," he said. "I should have realized it was you. Let me go get Natalia."

"That won't be necessary. I need the keys to my office and for business to start again as usual. Get them to wrap it up for now and save the rest for the last hour of the day. Time is money, and I intend for the company to make some today."

The man nodded and took off for the party.

I went back to the cubicle where I had left my belongings, and I opened my laptop and began organizing my days in fifteen-minute blocks. An organized man was an effective one, and few men were as productive as me.

I worked away for a while and placed an advertisement for a new personal assistant. I wanted the best of the best and made it clear in the ad that no one with less than five to ten years of experience working for a CEO should apply.

Feeling watched, I looked up and saw a mousy, nervous-looking woman clutching an armful of files. "Excuse me, sir, but this is my desk. I can point you in the direction of an unused one if you would like."

I gave her a baleful glare, and the woman dropped the files. Paper flew everywhere, some landing on top of my work and shoes.

"What is wrong with you!" I yelled at the top of my lungs. "Pick up this mess at once! How many projects have you delayed with your clumsiness?"

She stammered, "I-I don't know, sir. I had about forty files. It will take me a while to put things right, but I can do it. I just need some time," she said confidently. She got down on her hands and knees and began collecting papers.

"Who in the world is hollering over here?" came a soft and calm voice behind me.

The scent of lavender suddenly filled the air. I hated that scent. It reminded me of my mother. I turned to find the woman with the party hat still on her head.

"This is absolutely unacceptable. Since I came into this building, everything has been one disappointment after another. How is this company still operating? The staff members are a bunch of lazy idiots who would rather party than work, and when they do work, they're inept and clumsy. I should fire the lot of you."

"Cassius Baxter, I'm Natalia Blake." She held out her hand, and I did not take it.

"Great, Miss Blake, please open my office and give me all copies of the keys. Now."

The woman sighed. "Has anyone ever told you that you'll catch more flies with honey than vinegar?"

My glare could darken a room. But the woman did not seem affected by it.

"Give me ten minutes," she said, bending down to help the woman pick up the files.

"She can pick up those files by herself. Do as I ordered, or consider yourself fired without severance," I said through gritted teeth.

"Then fire me," she said, continuing to pick up the papers. "But I'm the only one available to help you run this company. And if I go, so do my clients. It was part of the stipulations I made with the former owner when accepting this promotion. Not to mention that firing me over this violates human resource laws."

"Natalia, was it?" I asked venomously. "I expect you to start applying for work elsewhere. You will receive severance, but I highly doubt you and I will be able to work together. At least, not with that attitude."

"I have an attitude?" She seemed shocked at the accusation. "I am not the one terrifying interns and ruining everyone's day by ordering them back to work. They earned this downtime, and I intend to see that they get it."

I felt my nails digging into my palms because my fists were clenching so hard. The nerve of this woman to challenge my directives. Just because she had a pretty face and a svelte body did not mean I would give in to her. I had a feeling she was used to getting her way with men. But I vowed to make sure she knew her place within a day.

"The keys, Miss Blake. Now."

This time, she stood and laid the files on top of the nearby desk. "Tracy? Can you manage the rest?"

"Yes, Miss Blake," Tracy said in a rush.

"Great work on the project, by the way," Natalia congratulated the girl. "Keep it up, and you won't be an intern for long."

Tracy eyed me uneasily from the corner of her eye. "Thank you, Miss Blake." She grabbed the rest of the files and rushed off toward an empty cubicle instead of asking for hers back.

Well, at least she was smart enough to do that. But this bitch of a woman, this Miss Blake, would be gone before the week was out. *Screw her and her clients,* I thought petulantly. The employees didn't need a nursemaid. What they needed was a leader. And this woman, with her soft ways, would not cut it.

"What's your new position?" I asked, wondering what role I would need to fill.

"I'm your vice president and CFO for the board of directors," she said, holding her head high.

"As I said, Miss Blake, begin job hunting."

She sighed, and I realized I did know this woman with her gorgeous long hair and big doe eyes. *Did I hook up with her already?* I wasn't quite sure, so I didn't bother recollecting. If we had gotten together before, it obviously hadn't been a life-changing event for me, so it was better left forgotten, especially considering her attitude and stubbornness. The woman was grating on my nerves, and I clench my jaw to keep from yelling at her.

She gave me a cool look but walked away, and I couldn't help but watch the sway of her hips as she left. *It's a shame,* I thought, turning back to my computer. *You don't see an ass like that every day.*

Chapter Three

NATALIA

I could not believe the arrogance and cruelty of the man I'd had a one-night stand with years ago. I was happy he didn't recognize me. That way, I wouldn't have to worry that he would put two and two together and find out about Bella. I would do anything in my power to keep that asshole from my child.

How dare he address poor Tracy with such rudeness and with blatant disregard for her feelings. This company would go to shit with that man at its head. And how dare he threaten me. I was irreplaceable. I had helped build this company to what it was today.

But already, I was missing my old boss. His passing had been hard for me. He had taken me under his wing when I was still an entry-level marketer and made me into one of the best in the country. Together we had built a client base of some of the biggest brands in the world.

My office was a few doors down from Cassius's new one. I had the keys for his, and I was loath to hand them over to Cassius. He deserved to struggle a bit. He had probably been handed everything his whole life.

When I'd walked away, I had felt his eyes on me, and it felt like spiders crawling up my back. I prayed that he wouldn't recognize me. I went into my office and began planning how I could prove myself to him. I was waiting to see how this whole situation panned out. Maybe Cassius had just given me the wrong impression. He had been genial enough when we'd had sex all those years ago. But then again, he probably had just been nice to get laid.

I looked at the picture on my desk of Bella and me. We were cuddled up on the couch. Rory had taken it when she was just a baby. I wanted to hide the picture, so I slid it into the top drawer of my desk.

Someone knocked timidly on my door.

"Come in," I said loudly so they would hear me through my solid office door.

Tracy opened the door, peeking her head in. "Miss," she said, "the new CEO wants his keys, and I thought you might have them."

I sighed loudly. "Yes, I will deliver them to him."

Tracy gave me a conspiratorial smile. "Thank you for helping me earlier, miss. The man makes me so nervous."

"I don't blame you for feeling that way. He is very overbearing and ignorant, and I have a feeling that things are only going to get worse. But don't worry, Tracy. Just keep your head down, and do your work. I'll make sure you get the recognition you deserve."

Tracy gave me a sweet smile, then closed the door as she left.

I organized the work I had to do for the day, then figured I had made him wait long enough. Looking in my mirror, I fixed my makeup and straightened my dress. It hugged my curves and had a deep but professional neckline. I didn't have much in the way of breasts, but I knew I had a dancer's long legs. And my hips and ass were my best features, or so I had been told.

I stopped, realizing I was making sure I looked good. The man didn't deserve my prepping. I put the lipstick I was about to reapply in my purse and grabbed the office keys out of my desk. Walking confidently, I went down to face the man. When he saw the keys in my hand, his face darkened. I couldn't believe I had once found him so attractive. If I had known his real personality was like this, I wouldn't have slept with him in the first place. At least he wasn't in my daughter's life.

I dropped the keys on Tracy's desk. "I'm sorry it took so long to bring the keys," I said innocently. "I forgot where they were."

He snatched them off the desk. "Are these the only copies?"

It wasn't in my nature to lie, so I said yes.

"Come into my office, Miss... what's your name?"

"Nakita Blake," I repeated grudgingly.

He went to the office door and used the keys to open it.

"I have clients to attend to," I said, hoping to get out of whatever conversation he intended to have with me.

"They can wait." The door opened, and he strolled in, throwing down his bag and setting his computer on the large, antique desk.

"I want to discuss your behavior with you. It was totally unacceptable. First, you questioned my actions, and you better never do that to me again. And secondly, you let your underlings get away with murder. You should chastise them when they make mistakes. This is not a preschool. It's a multimillion-dollar business, and we will not allow subpar performances from our staff. Do you understand? Then to override what I said humiliated me. I am the CEO and owner. Not you."

I felt my face heat in silent rage. I didn't dare open my mouth for fear of what I might say. This man was a complete piece of shit. I was embarrassed that I had let him stick his cock in me. There was no way I would ever let him into Bella's life. The man was too heartless and demanding. Bella didn't need that sort of influence.

He repeated himself, "Do you understand, Miss Blake?"

I didn't answer. Instead, I turned around and walked toward the door, swinging my hips purposely to show Cassius what he would never have again.

"Get back here, or you're fired!" he screamed at me.

I slammed the door behind me. Half of the staff had stopped and were staring at me with their mouths open.

"Don't worry about it, guys," I reassured them. "I am not going anywhere."

Many of them looked doubtful, but they returned to their work. I stalked to my office and grabbed my purse and computer. I couldn't stay in this building for one more minute, and I figured I could let him think he scared me away. I walked to the elevator with my head held high.

When I got into the elevator, I let out a long sigh. The man was going to ruin the business. I didn't understand how such a man could become a billionaire. It must be because he was so selfish and tight-assed.

I broke out my cell phone and called Rory.

"Yello?" he answered with his weird greeting.

"You will never believe who now owns Prism Media," I said in a rush. I realized my heart was pumping hard in my chest. Cassius had upset me more than I thought. "It's Cassius Baxter. Bella's father." The elevator door opened, and I squeezed through a flood of people entering.

"You're kidding," he said, disbelief evident in his voice.

"I'm dead serious, Rory. And what's worse, he just tried to fire me."

"Did he fire you?" His voice was now full of worry.

"No," I said. "He can't. I have a significant stake in the company and am in charge of over half the clientele. If I leave, his business will fall into shambles. Plus, I would win a multimillion-dollar lawsuit if he tries, and he knows it."

"Jesus, Nat," Rory said, "are you worried he will find out about Bella?"

"No," I said. "He didn't even recognize me. I was likely just one of the hundreds of women he must have fucked in his lifetime."

"Well, that's good news, at least."

"I'll disappear into thin air if he does figure it out. There is no way I am letting that oaf into Bella's life. I'm on my way home. Do we need anything?"

"I don't think you should come home. I think you should stay and let Cassius know he can't order you around. Get lunch, then go back to your office. Also, aren't you supposed to have a party today for your promotion?"

"I totally forgot about that with all the chaos. You're right. I'm going to grab a bite to eat, and I'll finish the day whether he likes it or not."

"That's the spirit," he said.

I could tell he was grinning from the sound of his voice. I didn't know what I would have done without Rory all these years. He was the fatherly figure that Bella needed, not the arrogant asshole that Cassius Baxter was.

We hung up the phone, and I went for some sushi. I didn't want to fill up on too much food because I knew there was a cake and a potluck waiting for me back at the office. Once I finished, I resolutely walked back to work. Entering the building, I felt my palms sweat, and I was worried there might be a confrontation.

I didn't think I could hold my silence if the man hollered at me again. But when I reached the floor, everyone was silent. One of my coworkers raised his fist in the air as a salute when I walked by him. Then I saw money exchange hands. *So they bet on whether or not I would return, huh?*

It amused me, and I gave them all a big smile. I would not be scared off, and I would not back down from a tyrant. My staff needed me to speak for them, and I would not let them down. I purposely strolled casually by Cassius's office. He glared at me for a second and looked away like I wasn't there. I considered it a win.

Then, instead of waiting until the last hour of the day, I started the celebration up again after lunch. At first, the staff was hesitant, but soon, they were all laughing and dancing to music. I let myself relax and put back on the party hat. I also made sure to sample all the dishes they had made for the potluck. Soon I felt full and bloated, and I sat back and relaxed while they busted out the champagne for a toast.

"To Natalia," said Guy, "the best CFO and partner the company has even had."

The rest of the staff cheered.

Soon, it was the end of the workday, and several of the employees wanted to continue the party at a bar. I politely declined and dismissed them for the day. Then I went to my office to collect my belongings.

Cassius was leaning on the doorframe of his office. He watched me as I went by. "This isn't the end of it," he sneered. "I meant it when I said to look for new employment."

"I won't have to look for new employment. You need me. I am the most qualified employee for the role and directly handle over half of your clientele."

"You do not want to have me for an enemy, Miss Blake."

"You don't scare me, Cassius Baxter," I responded.

"You will. Just wait and see." He said it in a chilling voice, and I could hear the venom in his tone.

He did, in fact, scare me. But not for the reasons he thought. I knew he could make my life unpleasant, but it was him finding out about Bella and realizing who I was that I feared. I turned and walked away with a calm and relaxed façade. But deep inside, I could feel myself trembling.

Chapter Four

CASSIUS

The nerve of that woman, I thought, watching her as she walked to the elevators. She had a proud and confident step that I couldn't help but admire, especially the sensual way her hips swayed. Natalia was beautiful, and she knew it. I hated women who used their looks to badger men into getting their way. Deep down, all beautiful women were the same, especially my most recent ex, Tina.

That was a can of worms I wasn't ready to open right now, so I shoved the thought of the cheating slut out of my mind.

The worst thing was that Natalia Blake knew I couldn't fire her. She, indeed, was the glue that had held the company together while the former owner had ailed and eventually passed away. I read the contract the two of them worked up, and if I released her from her position, she could easily take over half the clients with her.

I sent a copy of the document to my lawyers, looking for a loophole, but so far, all they said was that it was ironclad. Her stake in the company was only 1 percent less than mine. The two of them had truly thought of everything. This legal agreement was not what I had expected when I took over the business.

From what I had heard, the former owner, Charlie, had groomed her for leadership from the day she started. She had risen through the ranks with her personable nature, a natural way with clients, and pure grit. In most cases, I would have loved to have someone like that by my side, but something about her threw me off. I couldn't explain it. It was like she hated me from the moment she saw me.

Most women flirted with me and treated me like I was a god. Her blatant disinterest and challenging nature rubbed me the wrong way. Maybe she was a lesbian. That would explain things.

I was glad the day was over, and it had gone so much worse than I had imagined it could. That woman had undermined me in every possible way. By setting herself against me, I knew that her loyal underlings would follow in her steps. I had to work this out, but I was too tired to focus. I closed my laptop and turned my phone back on.

I saw that I had twenty missed calls, all from Tina. I would have to change my number or find some way to block her, which would be very annoying. I wished I had an assistant already to deal with this hassle. During the day, I had found a few promising individuals and invited them for video interviews starting tomorrow. I was actually looking forward to it because finding talented individuals to bring to my empire brought me personal joy.

I yawned and went home, crashing on the sofa of my penthouse suite without even a bite to eat for supper.

The next morning I showered in the luxurious bathroom. The standup shower was large enough to hold ten people, with jets that hit from every angle. The bathroom was what had sold me on this building. *Why be a billionaire if I couldn't enjoy the finer things in life?* Feeling randy, I began jerking off in the shower. My cock was as hard as a rock, and I was surprised to find that it was responding to my thoughts of Natalia Blake.

I shook my head and thought of my favorite pornstar, but Natalia kept intruding on my mind. I imagined myself dominating her by throwing her over my lap and giving her hard spankings for her behavior. That perfectly heart-shaped ass and those wide hips were enough to drive a man mad with lust. I wasn't typically into S&M, but the idea of taking control of her both professionally and personally drove me wild.

Soon I was stroking my cock hard, imagining her taking the mushroom tip of my penis into that rosebud mouth of hers. I imagined her leaving red lip prints on my shaft as I gripped her hard by her cascading brown locks. It was weird. I felt like I had already experienced this before. I must have dreamed of the siren last night.

I pumped my cock harder and faster, feeling my muscles beginning to twitch. I let the water pour onto my groin, adding to the sensation. Then I convulsed, watching as my ejaculate sprayed into the air. I groaned, wishing I had been balls deep in Natalia's wet and waiting pussy.

I couldn't understand what drew me to the woman. Maybe it was how she had made me feel impotent the day before, but today would be different. I swore to myself.

When I left my building, my driver was waiting for me with a big grin on his face. I was shocked, as I did not have to call him this time. He just knew when to expect me. I took it as a good sign and hoped the rest of the day would be as pleasant. I didn't want to come off the way I had yesterday. I knew I had started on the wrong foot with the staff and that I would have to find a way back into their good graces.

It would be a challenge, but I had never backed down from one and wasn't about to start today. I entered the building and was met by a profound silence once the elevator door opened to the floor. Everyone seemed to be studiously working, but I could tell that the staff had likely been talking about me prior to my arrival. To throw them all off, I grinned maniacally.

A few returned my smile but then ducked their heads as if the pages or screens they were reading held the secrets to eternal life.

Then I saw her from across the room. Natalia hadn't seen me yet but was talking conspiratorily with an employee. I saw the papers in their hands, and I could see the respect the woman received from the employees.

As if she could feel my gaze, Natalia looked up with a vacant expression. If I didn't know that she had intellect, I would have almost said it was a vapid look. But she swiftly turned away and walked into her office.

So, I did the same. I opened the blinds to my office so I could watch the employees work and keep tabs on Miss Blake. The day went by slowly, and every time I looked at my watch, it seemed like only minutes had gone by. I took off my Rolex and put it in the top drawer of my desk.

Miss Blake went in and out of her office quite often to speak with a wide range of the staff. It seemed like she was the hands-on type, and I could respect her for that if she weren't such a pain in my ass. But Natalia didn't stop her efforts and involvement with the employees. I could tell she was a hard worker and dedicated to the company, but she should stay more aloof like me. Personal entanglements could get in the way of doing good business.

She would be more apt to let people slack off or forgive their many faults, which did not work in a billion-dollar company. I would have to outline what was acceptable and what wasn't. Under the previous owner, she'd had free reign, and that would stop now that I was in charge. Natalia Blake wouldn't like it, but I had to pull her down from her high horse before it worsened.

My desk phone rang, and I picked it up. I hadn't received a call on this line, so I was shocked.

"Hello?"

"Is this Mr. Baxter?"

"Yes, may I ask who's calling?"

"My name is Glenda Filch from *Poise* magazine. We heard that Prism Media is under new management and wish to cancel our contract with you effective immediately."

"May I ask why?" I asked, sincerely curious. I knew they were one of our biggest clients, and our company's advertisements for other brands took up the majority of their magazine's ads.

"We have decided to move in a new direction, and we're not sure your company will fit the picture."

They wanted more money from the situation. I could read between the lines.

"Give me a chance to change your mind. I will gather my colleagues and work on something more beneficial to our businesses."

"Time is of the essence, Mr. Baxter. You have until the end of the day." Then she rudely hung up on me without another word.

Poise magazine was an umbrella company with many different magazines produced by them. If we lost this, it would only be a matter of time before the companies that advertised in their magazines moved on to another marketing firm.

I pushed away from my desk, opened the office door, and hollered, "Get Miss Blake, now!"

I watched as the intern I'd intimidated the day before scurried to Natalia's office, banged hard on the door, and relayed the message.

Out stormed Natalia. By the expression on her face, she clearly did not like being summoned as she had been. She opened my office door without bothering to knock.

"If you need me in the future, I expect you to use the phone. Not scream for me and startle the employees. I am number one on the speed dial. What do you want?"

"*Poise* wants to pull out," I said calmly.

Her face paled. She knew exactly what that would mean for the business, and I was happy she was quick on the uptake.

"Call a meeting with our best people. We need a plan and a great idea to keep them with us."

"They're looking for a more profitable arrangement," she said, twirling her hair with a finger. Natalia looked distracted. "Charlie said they'd do it."

"And he didn't come up with a contingency plan?" I was pissed. *Shouldn't the man have arranged for it if he'd foreseen this happening?*

"He was a little busy dying." Sarcasm and loathing dripped from her lips.

I chose to ignore her sarcasm.

"Get the team together. Meet in the boardroom. We are going to work until we come up with a solution." She rolled her eyes but left my office in a hurry.

In ten minutes, the employees filled the boardroom seats, and many of the faces were deeply concerned.

I walked to the end of the table and went to the whiteboard. "Who has an idea for how we can keep *Poise* as a client and publisher?"

The room was so silent I could have sworn I heard heart rates increase. No one raised a hand, and no one said a word.

"What the hell is wrong with you people? Are you a bunch of idiots? Pitch me ideas. It's what we pay you for."

Then Natalia walked into the room. She wore a red dress suit, fire-truck red pumps, and had lusciously painted crimson lips. She looked so hot that I wanted to take her right there on the board-room table. The woman sure knew how to dress and flaunt her features. The way that suit hugged her curves reminded me of how I'd jerked off to her this morning. I felt the bulge in my pants grow and sat down to hide it.

I turned toward her. "What is the plan, Vice President?"

She scowled slightly at me before turning toward the gathered employees. "I don't think we will need any idea-pitching from the staff. What we need are our lawyers, and I will handle them person-ally. I intend to bring our team of legal professionals and arrive at their office with their contracts. I have already arranged for the lawyers to review the documents. Get back to work. Mr. Baxter and I will handle things."

"That's not much of a plan," I said skeptically. But if it didn't work, all the blame would be shifted to her, and that didn't bother me in the least.

"It's a matter of money, Mr. Baxter, and as chief financial officer, that is within my purview."

I didn't think I could trust her with something this major. I was left sitting alone in the boardroom, wondering. *Would she work for the company's benefit or her own?*

Natalia Blake turned toward me. "I'll have this sorted by the end of the day, and I recommend you relax and think about other things." Then she sauntered out of the room, practically brimming with confidence.

All I knew for sure was that we were on a ship, and an iceberg had appeared straight ahead. *Would we rise and shine or sink and rust?* All I knew was that I had a pit in my stomach and Miss Natalia Blake was the cause of it.

Chapter Five

NATALIA

The way Cassius Baxter looked at me when I entered the boardroom was full of doubt and concern. I couldn't help but scowl at him. It was not proper behavior to demonstrate in a room full of employees, but I quickly pushed the thought out of my head. I had bigger fish to fry.

I turned and expressed my needs and exuded confidence that I could handle the issue with *Poise* magazine by myself. I knew they didn't really want to pull out. It was just a scare tactic to weasel their way into making more money from the company and the brands we catered to. That would not do, and I fully intended to make *Poise* regret their threats.

We brought them millions of dollars in revenue through our advertisements, and they wouldn't let go of one of the most talented teams in the industry. The fact that they called Cassius instead of me demonstrated they were trying to figure out the new power structure in the company. I would soon be correcting their mistake if they assumed I was just going to sit back and let the new boss handle everything.

For a "progressive" woman-run company, they sure had tried to keep me out of the issue. I am sure that Glenda Filch had done her best to make herself known to Cassius while at the same time pressuring him for her company's benefit. She was brilliant at what she did, but she didn't realize that I was better. I aimed to drag even more contracts from her before the end of the day and show *Poise* that they were not the only option in the magazine industry. Sure, we would have to adjust to a new style with new concepts, but I had complete faith in my team. They were the best of the best. That was why we hired them.

And Charlie had prepared a contingency plan. On my desk lay portfolios and storyboards for taking over the male magazine industries. If we couldn't beat the female magazines down, then we would focus on the men.

We would need to hire more professionals to work on male-driven projects, but I knew they could do it with guidance and coaching. I gathered my storyboards for current projects with *Poise*, made sure our legal team was at the magazine's headquarters, and brought the storyboards for male magazines to demonstrate that we would only be expanding from here. That would put their faith back in us. I was sure of it.

My neck felt stiff as I walked to the elevators with a leap in my step. I had a good feeling about today. Everything was clicking together, and Cassius had given me complete control, but I believed it was because he wanted to watch my failures if things didn't work out. The man was shrewd, and he kind of reminded me of what I had been like when I had first joined Prism Media.

But I pushed him out of my thoughts and focused on the task at hand. In about half an hour, I was seated in the waiting room of *Poise* with three of our lawyers, all of whom were grinning like sharks, and I felt even more confident. What Glenda had done was a breach of a contract. By not consulting with the company as a whole, instead discussing it with the new CEO, she had nullified the agreement. By sharing private information with Cassius, who was not present for or even fully aware of the relationship with

Poise, Glenda had discussed private matters with someone who was technically a third party.

Charlie had thought of everything, including who she had to talk to about contract changes, which was me. I had her by the scruff of her neck, and I would shake her until loose change came out.

When the door to her office opened, Glenda's face was pale, and she swung the door wide and waved us in.

The lawyers did the talking while I sat there smiling like the Cheshire cat. Her team of lawyers scrambled to keep ahead of things, but soon they were advising her to renew the contract or face monetary penalties.

"I think I'll accept the penalties and find another marketing company to collaborate with." Her answer shocked me.

"Listen, Mrs. Filch. We are prepared to pull out and focus on the male magazine industry." I presented the portfolio and showed her the preliminary steps we were already taking.

"As the new vice president of the company and our CFO. I have been planning on expanding our reach. We wanted to create a mutually beneficial collaboration between *Poise* and the male magazine industry. Cross marketing so that even your company will benefit."

I could tell I had her attention now. I could practically see dollar signs in her eyes.

"Together, we could build an empire and dominate the whole magazine industry. I would think that would interest you, but if you are willing to pull out, please do so. We will continue with this plan with or without your consent or help. Though I believe your board of directors would look favorably upon this offer."

Glenda tapped her purple acrylic nails on the tabletop. She eyed one of the lawyers, and I saw a brief nod of his head. The lawyers looked interested.

Then Glenda said, "We are intrigued, but we want to work out the deal and the legal contract today."

I had them. I smiled widely and shook Glenda's hand. "I'm glad you came around. *Poise* is one of our best collaborators, and we would have hated to lose what you bring to the table."

We spent the rest of the day working out the specifics, then I called Cassius. "I did it. They're in."

"How did you manage that?" he asked, seeming genuinely interested, but also slightly skeptical.

"Before Charlie passed away, we had been making plans on working with the male magazine industry. I brought out storyboards and our portfolio of ideas, and Glenda changed her mind. She knows the revenue will bring in millions, and she couldn't pass it up."

"Congratulations. We will plan a celebration in the office for tomorrow. Have a good evening, Miss Blake."

I couldn't help but smile. I had shown him my value, and even more surprisingly, he wanted to celebrate my success. It shocked me, but any improvement in our relationship was a step forward. And I knew the exact dress I wanted to wear.

I left *Poise* and picked up Bella from day care. We went for ice cream and played at the park. Then we went home and made supper with Rory. The three of us ended the evening watching cartoons and cuddling on the couch. It was precisely how I wanted to spend the evening, and Bella and I fell asleep on the sofa, entwined in each other's arms.

The following day, I took extra care with my appearance. Rory had bought me a silver minidress that sparkled. When I'd first seen it, I had thought it was too distracting, but when I put it on, I found that it fit me snugly and accentuated my curvy hips. I put on a pair of black pumps, brushed and straightened my long brown hair, and used my silver and dark-gray eyeshadow to create a smokey eye. For my lips, I chose a dark-plum color. Pleased with my appearance, I wanted to show everyone that I was a woman to contend with, not some wallflower who had gotten lucky.

When I walked into the office, everyone suddenly popped up

from their desks, and a roar of approval and clapping hands nearly deafened me. Two coworkers rolled out a massive cake lit with sparklers. I felt proud of myself and happy that the employees were celebrating my success. This contract was the start of a new era for the business, and I was leading the way.

Then I saw Cassius. He had come out of his office and wore a wry grin on his face, but there was heat in his eyes. I couldn't help but blush, remembering the night we had shared so long ago.

I wondered how different I looked compared to when I first started here at Prism Media. I had been a self-conscious mousy woman who had grown under the tutelage of the late CEO. Now I could afford and took the time for self-care. Charlie had taught me that appearing confident and professional was half the battle, and I had taught myself how to do my hair and makeup and had taken the time to shop for professional attire with a bit of sexiness added in. I found it made men underestimate me, which was a significant advantage in this industry.

Cassius casually strolled up to me and shook my hand. "Great job, Miss Blake. Now it's time to put your money where your mouth is. Can you live up to your agreements?"

"Mr. Baxter, I will be contacting several magazines and corporations later today to set up meetings."

"Excellent," he said, "did you contact them before you made this agreement with *Poise*, or was it a bluff?"

"I'll never tell," I said with a grin and walked toward the cake, shaking hands and accepting congratulations and hugs.

Cassius called out, "I hired a catering service to bring us lunch, and we will be having a half day today. If you choose to stay, there will also be an open bar."

The staff cheered even louder. I could see what Cassius was doing. He was trying to win them over. The fact that Cassius had made an effort surprised me, but it was also pleasant to see his stern demeanor fade away. Maybe he wasn't so bad after all. I watched as he disappeared into his office. Someone passed me a piece of cake, and I went and made some phone calls to some of the top men's magazines in the industry. The majority of them wanted to meet with us within a week, and I cleared my schedule to meet their demands.

Out of the ten magazines I called, eight were considering our offer. It was more than I had expected because, in truth, I had been bluffing with *Poise*. The contingency plan had been put in place as a last-ditch effort, and I was surprised at how well it had worked. Charlie had indeed been a mastermind. A tear dropped from my eye in memory of him. He would be so proud.

A knock came on my door, and I called for them to enter. In walked Cassius, his bearing regal, and I hadn't realized how tall he was until he was looming above me.

"Have a seat," I said, gesturing to one of the chairs. Cassius sat down and looked at me with the predatory eyes of an eagle.

"How did your calls go?"

"Better than I expected. We have eight magazines interested in what we have to offer, and I told them we were expanding and that we had great opportunities for those who jumped on board quickly. So, I suggest you clear your schedule, boss."

"Will do," he said, then he sniffed the air. "What perfume are you wearing? It smells familiar."

I froze. I wasn't wearing perfume. "I'm not sure," I said, waving the question away. Instead, I said, "Good work with the staff," to change the subject.

Cassius paused for a second. "I know how I can come off to people sometimes. We are a team, and I need things between us to work smoothly. What you did was excellent, and you deserve the position and title you have. I regret not treating you fairly."

He seemed genuine, so I said, "Don't worry about it. I want our professional relationship to work seamlessly, and we need to be working together, not butting heads."

He smiled at me and stood. "You look lovely today, Miss Blake." Then he turned and left my office.

I could tell he was trying to disarm me, but still I doubted whether or not his praise was genuine. Men like Cassius would do everything to mollify a woman, and he didn't have me fooled. I opened my desk drawer and took out the picture of Bella and me. I could not believe that he was the father of my child. He didn't deserve either of us, and I knew that I would never tell him he was a dad, no matter what happened.

Chapter Six

CASSIUS

A week later, I received a call from one of the leading erotic men's magazines. They offered to fly me in and treat a guest and me to a three-day all-expenses-paid trip at a snazzy resort up north, where winter was just releasing its hold on the countryside. The resort held indoor pools, outdoor hot tubs, and a fully operational spa, where guests could get massages, treatments, and a wide range of services almost any time of day.

They also had a glass room that held a gym so the athletes could look at the mountains. There were also trails to hike, canoes and kayaks, fishing and hunting expeditions to sign up for. But as I was coming for business, I didn't expect to get any vacationing done—just hard work to strike a deal with a very influential men's magazine enterprise.

I wondered who I should bring as a guest. It would be best if it were someone with excellent negotiating skills, and the first person that came to mind was Natalia Blake. The drop-dead gorgeous woman could make a man's heart flutter or stop with just a smile. She would be perfect. Not only for her negotiating skills but how she might use her looks to disarm the men. Women were always doing things like that, I thought.

I called her. "Hi, Natalia. This is Cassius."

"Hi," she said concernedly. "Is something wrong?"

"No, why would you think that?" I was confused.

"You usually address me as Miss Blake, that's all. What's up?"

I explained to her about our mini-vacation, and she was on board in a minute. This was the client she had wanted most, but due to their company catering to men, they had made it known that they wanted to speak directly to the male CEO.

I suddenly doubted my choice of who should attend the meeting with me but figured that the men would come to recognize that she always brought her game face to the table. She had won *Poise* back through pure grit and determination, and I knew she would put enough effort in to help close this deal.

"I have storyboards for the meeting and a portfolio of concept art. We want to give the male industry a more modern kick to meet the younger generations while still representing the older readers of the magazine."

I could tell by her description that the magazines would be more receptive once they saw the extent of her planning. I had to admire that in the woman. She was professional to the core and extremely good at getting what she wanted. The only thing that bothered me deep down was the fact that she did not seem to want or need me at all.

We hung up, and my new assistant, Vera, made up the itinerary for the trip. The woman was in her early forties and was quickly becoming my favorite PA. I didn't even have to ask her to do anything. She had made herself at home at a desk outside my office with her collection of cacti, then began topping up my coffee mug and suggesting the tools and equipment she required. She returned with an itemized list and where to get things the cheapest yet the highest quality. I gave her a company card and told her to get what she needed. I couldn't help but admire her frugality.

The weekend came faster than expected, and I found myself excited to go on the trip. I had to admit that part of it was about getting to know Natalia Blake a bit more. She remained a mystery partly because of how she showed no interest in me. It was probably the reason I felt myself slowly becoming attracted to her. I pushed the thoughts away. She was my business partner. That was it, despite what my fantasies shoved in my head.

We boarded the private jet and sat across from each other. She was abnormally quiet, and I noticed she had a locket on that I had never seen her wear before. Natalia kept playing with it, looking introspective. I let her be, closed my eyes, and took a nap. I woke to Natalia kicking my shoe.

"We're here," she said.

We both stood simultaneously and were so close to each other that I could feel the warmth of her body and smell that exotic scent she seemed to have.

"Excuse me," I said, moving away from her quickly and grabbing my carry-on from the overhead container. I pulled her bag down as well and handed the compact pink suitcase to her.

"Thank you," she said and began making her way off the plane.

A limo waited on the tarmac for us, and we entered the vehicle then took the hour-long drive up to the Broadmoor Resort in the mountains of Colorado.

I saw Natalia's eyes light up when she saw the resort. It was impressive. I began hoping for more free time so Natalia and I could enjoy the various pools, spas, and other activities.

She narrowed her eyes and left me behind as she strolled up to the resort's entrance.

I caught up with her quickly, and soon we were booked into our separate rooms. We were due to meet the clients in an hour, and Natalia went to her room to clean up and dress for the meeting. I decided to head to the gift shop and explore the facilities. The place was truly marvelous, and I found out that we could go on several adventures. Zip lining looked fun, and I wondered if I could convince Natalia to try it.

When she came down the stairs from her suite, my mouth

dropped open. She was immaculate in a fuchsia dress. The dress was bare in the back to just above her hips but had a very modest front up to her collarbone. She wore black shoes and had her hair up in a twist, with dangling silver earrings and a locket for adornment. She also had a silver tennis bracelet on.

I went to greet her and led the way to the conference room. Six men sat in the chairs, and all stood when she entered. When she finally was seated, everyone sat down. We all introduced ourselves, then Natalia began her presentation. I had no idea she had set up a slide show of her plans for the magazine and its affiliates. I was pleased to see nodding heads and impressed looks on the men's faces.

She discussed the financial goals and estimates and the additional staff she would need to take care of the new clients. She had everything covered. I sat there feeling useless. But it was her time to shine, and her excitement as she discussed the process was infectious. We were served lobster bisque for our midday meal, then adjourned the meeting. The lawyers were set to arrive tomorrow, and we had accomplished so much in this one meeting that we expected to be finished a day early.

Tomorrow would be spent handling the contracts and agreements. When we all stood, there were a lot of happy faces and handshaking.

It was basically over. We had attained a vast corporate client that would bring in more revenue than *Poise*. And it was all due to Natalia and her hard work. I was beginning to see the woman in a new light, and she was slowly gaining my respect.

Heading up to my suite, I put on my swimming trunks and went to the indoor pool to do laps. I missed the regular workout routine that I did every morning and needed to make up for that. When I reached the end of the lane, Natalia was sitting on the edge of the pool. She wore a gold bikini and gave me a huge smile.

I grinned back at her. "You did a wonderful job today."

"Thank you," she said demurely, looking down as if shy from the praise.

"What are you doing for the evening?" I asked, pulling myself out of the water to sit next to her.

"I was thinking about dining in one of the restaurants, then having a massage. My neck is killing me. They also have this hot rock treatment I've always wanted to try."

I nodded. "Well, if anyone deserves to treat themselves to a little self-care, it's you. But I was wondering if you would like to try one of the adventure packages the resort offers."

"Like what?" she asked, kicking her feet gently in the water.

"They have this package called the Soaring Adventure. It's made up of zip lines, rope bridges, and rappelling. I guess the views are magnificent, and you get to view this canyon with beautiful waterfalls. I think it would be thrilling and fun. What do you think?"

"It sounds amazing. I would love to do it. Sign us up," she said excitedly.

"Do you have appropriate clothing for something like that?" I asked, looking at her bikini speculatively.

She slapped my shoulder gently. "Of course I do. I am not an idiot. I expected some downtime when I didn't have to be dressed up."

With chagrin, I smiled at her. "Sorry."

"Don't worry about it," she murmured.

"Would you like to have dinner with me, Miss Blake?"

"Oh, so we're back to the usual formalities. I was worried for a second. I thought you might be sick or something," she teased.

"Healthy as a horse," I said, pounding on my chest with a fist.

She rolled her eyes dramatically.

"What type of food are you in the mood for?" I asked.

"Steak. I want one medium-rare, and I heard they have an excellent restaurant that makes them perfectly."

"All right," I said.

Natalia rested her hand on my shoulder and boosted herself up. Looking down at me, she winked and walked to the exit. I watched her ass jiggle with every step. Gold never looked so good.

The dinner went well. She talked to me about our employees and who she expected to rise through the ranks. She knew the staff so well, and I couldn't figure out who half the people were that she spoke about. But I didn't stop her from carrying on. Her passion for her underlings was something I couldn't relate to.

Afterward, she said goodnight to me and went to the spa.

The thought of Natalia and her scent continued to fill my head. Not only was I starting to respect her, I was also becoming attracted to her. I pushed the thought aside. She was my business partner. That was it.

I was so tired I crawled into bed in my clothes and passed out.

Chapter Seven

NATALIA

After my spa treatments last night, I felt terrific. They had buffed and polished every layer of my skin, and the registered massage therapist managed to get the aggravating kink out of my neck. I'd never felt better. And that heated stone treatment had seeped out all the tension I hadn't even known I was holding in my body.

I also got a manicure and pedicure. Not to mention, I got a hair trim and cut long layers into my locks. When I began dressing for the meeting, I took out the burgundy suit and skirt I had planned for that day. I used little makeup. Instead, I just highlighted my features with some light mascara and eyeliner. I rubbed a dark lip stain into my lips, making me look like I had been eating a pomegranate.

Deciding to leave my hair down, I braided two front sections of my hair, then wrapped them around like a crown. I liked the effect, and it felt regal. I used a few bobby pins to keep it in place, then smiled at the reflection in the mirror.

Today, I thought, *I'm going to close the second major deal in my career, and I will be considered the best in the industry and bring in profits I've only dreamed of.*

The lawyers were due to arrive shortly, so I exited my beautiful suite and went down to meet them, Cassius, and the six board members. Everyone looked so positive that I could practically squeal with glee. Even Cassius wore a rare smile.

It didn't take us long to bang out the fine details. Everyone wanted to finish as early as possible so we could take advantage of what the resort had to offer. One man was planning on going fly fishing, so I discussed the zip lining adventure Cassius, and I would do this afternoon. After that, everyone seemed to want to sign up for it.

The lawyers disappeared to write up and print all the legal documents to be ready for our signatures later in the evening, or the following morning, depending on what they managed to get finished.

Meanwhile, we ate a wonderful buffet meal in the outdoor gazebo. I was amazed at the selection. I didn't overeat, though. I was a bit afraid of heights, and the last thing I wanted to do was vomit on someone. Afterward, Cassius and I excused ourselves and went to our suites to get dressed for the excursion.

I wore a pink tracksuit and a pair of white sneakers. Tying my long hair up into a messy bun, I left the braids as they were. It was a cute look, and I decided I would wear my hair like this more often. My makeup had stayed on remarkably well, and I knew it was due to the new eye and facial primers I had bought. I decided to leave my makeup and went down to the foyer to find Cassius.

As I came down the stairs, I saw him in a blue T-shirt and a pair of jeans. I had never seen him in jeans before, and it caught me off guard. He looked good. When he turned and saw me, he gave me a dazzling smile.

I approached him, and he said, "What's with you and pink?"

I shrugged, not wanting to tell him it was because it was his daughter's favorite color. "Am I late?" I asked to avoid the subject.

"No, we're right on time." He pointed to a group gathering around a man holding a clipboard.

We followed him out of the resort and headed to where the zip lines started. We got clipped and tied into harnesses and were given helmets and gloves for protection. I thought it was pretty weak protection if we were going to fall, but I tried not to think about that.

I could feel my adrenaline begin to rise. I was really going to do this. "Hey, Cassius?" I asked to get his attention. "Can you take lots of pictures for me? My cousin won't believe I did this if I don't have photographic evidence."

He grinned. "No problem. I brought my GoPro." He pointed to his helmet, and I saw he had a camera strapped to it.

"Excellent!" I said. "You have to send the whole thing to me after."

Then the man running the excursion said, "Get in line."

I felt panicky somewhat and started to tremble.

Cassius looked at me with a raised eyebrow. "Are you going to be okay, Natalia?"

"Of course," I lied. I entered the lineup behind Cassius and took a few deep breaths. *I can do this,* I told myself. And before I knew it, it was my turn.

Cassius looked back at me with a big grin as he started down the zip line. Then I was strapped in, and they pushed me to get started. I held on tight as if my life depended on it. But then the feeling of the open air and the rush as I was propelled forward made me feel like I was flying.

Oddly enough, it was like these lucid dreams that I often had where I would fly. It felt freeing, and all the anxiety I had been holding melted away. I looked at the beauty of the canyon. The striations of the rocks were stunning with the browns, reds, and whites.

And then I saw the towering waterfall. It was awe-inspiring as it cascaded down the cliff face. I looked at Cassius and was shocked to see that he was watching me. Then I realized he was pointing his GoPro at me. I waved, then let go of my death grip on the ropes and leaned back, extending my arms. The rush of adrenaline made goose bumps break out on my skin. I felt amazing, but I grabbed the rope again and continued to make my way down the zip line.

The adventure package definitely lived up to the hype. When I reached the other end of the line, they unhooked us, and I was bouncing around, full of energy like a live wire. When Cassius was near, I wrapped my arms around him and hugged him. By the look on his face, he was surprised.

"Thanks so much for making me do this. It is awesome!" I said, hoping that he didn't mind the random hug.

"No problem," he said. "But we aren't done. We have rope bridges to cross, then a cliff face to rappel down." His excitement was evident. His grin reminded me of a young boy's. He looked years younger when he smiled. It was too bad he didn't smile more often.

We began to walk along the bridges. They moved with each step, and I had difficulty walking on them until I found the rhythm. Cassius was only a bit ahead of me but would turn around sometimes to catch me on video.

I couldn't believe I had the guts to do this. We passed by so close to the cliff face that I reached out and touched the cool rock. I wished I could take a chunk of it but knew they would frown upon doing so. It wasn't long before we were at the cliff. I looked down, and my heart was in my throat. That was a long drop.

They strapped us into gear again and gave a demonstration on how to rappel down the cliff face. I paid close attention. When Cassius went to go ahead of me, I tapped him on the shoulder. "Do you mind if I go down first?"

He stepped aside and waved me forward. I got into position then leaned back and kicked off the cliff face. I dropped instead of taking measured steps and felt my stomach lurch, so I began making a slower progression down. It was exhilarating.

Soon I was at the bottom. I took off my gear and watched Cassius drop down the cliff in five massive jumps. He had obviously done this before. He hit the ground and took off his gear. Then came over to me with his GoPro in his hands. "I'll send you all the videos when I get to my computer. I got some pretty amazing shots."

"Thanks, I appreciate that," I said. I could feel my adrenaline was still sky-high. By the look in Cassius's blue eyes, I could tell he felt the same. Oddly enough, I felt like I didn't want to leave him just yet. We had shared an incredible experience, and it was almost as if we had formed a bond.

"Wanna grab a bite to eat, then hit the bar?" he asked. "Or maybe go sit in the hot tub?"

"Yeah, sure," I said. "We can do something. I am just not sure what."

He raised a quizzical eyebrow. Cassius was very expressive with his eyebrows, I absentmindedly noticed.

"I have a massive Jacuzzi in my suite. We could order room service, drink from the minibar, and sit in the tub," he suggested. "With our swimsuits on, of course."

Now it was my turn to give him a quizzical look. His face was the picture of innocence.

"I guess," I said, feeling a bit nervous. I was more comfortable with Cassius, but I wasn't sure about the depth of comfort. I clutched my locket containing a picture of Bella inside.

"It's just a suggestion," he said, clearly reading my discomfort.

"No," I said, "let's do it. I need to stop and get a swimsuit." He gave me another winning smile, and he was clearly delighted by my acceptance of his offer.

I went to my suite and stripped down, then pulled out my gold bikini. I switched it up for my teal one with a thong that showed off my ass. I don't know why I chose this one, but it felt right for some reason.

As I put it on, I reflected that this man was the father of my child, and I never expected to be with him or even see him again. Yet here we were, about to climb in a Jacuzzi together.

I had to admit that watching his thigh muscles and ass work as he made his way down the cliff face had turned me on a bit. I was beginning to see him in a sexual light again, and I couldn't wrap my head around whether or not this was a good thing. I was about to take the bikini off but felt foolish for being so indecisive. Grabbing a big, fluffy towel, I wrapped it around myself as I made my way to his suite.

He opened the door and handed me a menu. "I'm starving," he said as he walked to the sofa and sat down. He was wearing swim trunks, and I couldn't help but admire his pecs and washboard abs. I felt a bit lewd, as this was my coworker.

"What are you in the mood for?"

Sex. The thought came to my mind unbidden. It was followed by a sudden urge to get the hell out of there.

Chapter Eight

CASSIUS

Natalia looked lovely, wrapped in a plush towel. The teal color of her bikini top looked nice against the tan of her soft-looking skin. I wanted to reach out and touch her, but I had to remind myself that we were coworkers.

She sat down in the chair across from me, and I got up to serve her a drink. "What's your poison?" I asked, waving at the selection of hard liquor bottles.

"Rum and Coke, please," she said in a clipped voice.

I poured a double for her, and she took the glass and clutched it with two hands.

She took a sip and nodded. "It's perfect, thank you."

"Would you like to get in the Jacuzzi right away, or should we sit and chat for a while?"

"I have no preference. Either way suits me fine." She took another sip of her drink. "I'm not usually a drinker," she commented, "but this is going down smooth." She tilted her head back and downed the contents of the glass. "Can I have another?"

"Need a little liquid courage?" I asked teasingly.

She flushed, and I knew I was right on the money.

"Here," I said, handing her another drink. "I'm just joking.

What do you want to eat?" I asked, changing the subject so she didn't become even more uncomfortable.

"Chicken wings and a Caesar salad, please. Make that a chicken Caesar salad. I love chicken—nectar of the gods."

I couldn't help but chuckle. "Now I know your secret."

Her eyes widened, and a very subtle look of fear passed over her face. It was in the eyes. *Does she have something to hide?*

I clarified, "I'll bring you a whole chicken the next time I make you mad." Yes, there was relief in her chocolate-colored eyes. I tried not to look at her suspiciously. After my ex Tina and my best friend, Terry, cheated on me together, I had a hard time trusting anyone, but I hadn't always been like this, as hard as that was for me to imagine.

Focusing back on my guest and providing her with suitable entertainment, I sat on the couch again, picking up the phone and dialing room service. I ordered our meals, then was at a loss for what to say. That was very unlike me, but the silence stretched out.

"I wonder if they'll serve us in the Jacuzzi?" She tapped her chin thoughtfully.

"I highly doubt that. The hotel staff does have to maintain the place, and I doubt they want chicken bones in the drains."

"I have always wanted to eat chicken in a jet tub."

I couldn't tell if she was serious or not, so I grinned. "Looks like you will attain your dream tonight."

"I am truly blessed," she said, loosening the towel. "The rum is making me feel warm."

She lowered the towel, and it was my turn to blush. She was truly magnificent, and I had this odd feeling like I had been through this song and dance with her before. But I had to be mistaken.

"Do you need a refill?"

"Please," she said, handing me the empty glass.

I got up and was happy I had an excuse to stop gawking at her.

I was beginning to feel like a pervert. But she looked so exquisite that I couldn't help but admire her physical attributes.

Her skin looked like a dark cream liqueur, and her eyes were multi-faceted milk- and dark-chocolate brown. Her wavy hair cascaded over her shoulders, making the teal of her bikini top stand out against the teak hue. It was odd seeing her so casual and not as the respectable businesswoman that I knew she was.

She was still prim and proper, but her smile was more relaxed and her eyes hooded. It was likely the drinks, but I liked it. I tossed my drink back and refilled our glasses again. If we kept at the rate we were drinking, we wouldn't make it through the meal, so I made these drinks a single.

"Can you play some music?" she asked.

"Of course," I said, grabbing my phone. I saw a message from my ex Tina, and I ignored it. "I listen to classic rock mostly. But I'll listen to whatever you like."

"Are you assuming I don't enjoy classic rock?" Her smile was wry.

"Nothing of the sort," I assured her. "I imagine you have eclectic tastes and like a little bit of everything."

"All right," she said, setting her hand on the curve of her hip. "Play me your favorite song."

"That's easy." I turned on "One" by Metallica.

"That song is very morose," she commented.

I nodded, agreeing with her. "Very much so. But I find it eerily beautiful. There's some deep meaning to those words, and they are very personal and relatable. I think, some days, I used to listen to it just because it irritated my mother and father. But now, well, I feel the bite of those lyrics." My words trailed off.

She was eyeing me speculatively. "Cassius," she remarked, "from the outside looking into your world, it seems like you have the picture-perfect life that everyone dreams of, with wealth, prestige, and an Ivy League education. You are living the American dream."

"Can we change the topic, please? The last thing I want to think about on our one day off is my upbringing."

She shrugged and apologized, "Sorry. I didn't mean to pry."

"You weren't prying. No worries."

She didn't know of the isolation I had truly felt growing up as I did. I didn't have the warm and perfect life my family pretended it was. I pushed the thoughts away.

She got up, dropping her towel accidentally. When she bent to pick it up, she spilled her drink on her chest, interrupting the process. The liquid coated her modest chest, and the teal of her bikini darkened. But what had me standing still in shock was that there was no back to her bikini bottoms. Instead, a thong was squeezed between two round cheeks, and they were a sight of perfection. Every woman wanted that kind of ass.

I looked away before she could see my open-mouthed gaze. I knew I was blushing and pretended to be looking up music on my phone.

"I have to go wash this off and change my swimsuit. Do you want to come?"

Did I ever.

I scooped up her towel off the floor and followed her like a baby duckling out of the room, the room service completely forgotten. *What am I doing?* I purposely didn't look at her ass as she strolled down the hall with purpose. She must be feeling the alcohol.

She turned around and gave me a brilliant grin. "You know," she started, "I think I may be a little bit drunk already."

"I'm cool with it." *Why did I say that?* I wanted to smack my head into a wall.

She pulled the key card out of her bikini top and opened the door to her suite. Everything was pristine, as if the maid had just been in.

Natalia walked over to where her suitcase sat open on a stand.

She grabbed a violet-colored bathing suit, then walked into the bedroom. I followed her inside. *Is this really happening?*

"Could you please undo my ties and then turn on the shower? I am all sticky, and I can't stand that feeling on my hands."

"Sure," I said, hopping to the task.

Natalia held her hands away from her body, fingers splayed. At first, I thought she was just making an excuse to have me near her, but then I realized that she must have a bit of obsessive-compulsive disorder or something. I pulled the ties, and the bikini top dropped. But when I pulled the ties on the thong, it stayed where it was between her supple cheeks. I pulled it out, and it fell to the floor.

I was rock-hard. She looked down as if reading my thoughts, and a small smile danced on her lips. She sauntered to the bathroom, entrancing me with each sway of her wide-set hips. Then I remembered she had asked me to turn on the taps. I raced ahead of her and turned on the shower, adjusting the knobs until it reached a suitable temperature.

She stepped inside and was soon glistening under the fall of the water. "Care to join me?"

I didn't bother answering and stripped off my trunks. I grabbed a bar of soap off the counter and climbed in with her. We stood very close to each other, and I began lathering the soap in my hands.

We didn't speak, as if it might break the spell. With soapy hands, I started rubbing Natalia's sticky chest. Each apple-sized breast was tipped with a dark nipple. I rolled them through my fingers and bent my head to kiss her rose-petal lips.

Her tongue entered my mouth, and I could taste the rum. I briefly worried that she would regret this in the morning, but I couldn't bring myself to care for long. She was enchanting me with the small movements of her body. Like the delicate touch of her hand on my shoulder and how she rocked into my groin slowly, pressing my cock between our bellies.

I started rubbing down her stomach. She did not have ab muscles standing out, and instead, she had a soft and slightly protruding abdomen. I made circles around her belly button before sliding my fingers down to spread her nether lips.

The lubrication of the soap on my fingers made the motion slick, and I slid in easily between the folds, finding the nub of her clitoris. With circular motions, I rubbed her as our lips and breaths meshed. Her small hand found my cock and began stroking it, sending jolts of electricity through my groin.

I couldn't believe things had come to this. The way she had been with me, I thought she hated me. Yet here we were, and the sexual tension had me panting for more. I wanted to sheath myself in her tiny hole. I slid a finger inside of her then another. Then I began slowly removing them and reinserting them over and over. I could feel her natural lubrication, and my cock twitched in her hand in response.

She pulled her mouth away and started nipping at my collarbone. The motion felt familiar, and I had a weird sense of déjà vu. I pulled away, my hand slipping out from inside of her. I looked into her eyes and was sure that I had been this intimate with her before. *But was it in a dream?*

Natalia bit her lip and looked like she would say something but hesitated. Then she kissed me again, guiding my penis toward her waiting slit. I picked her up and wrapped her legs around me, sliding my cock inside. She was tight and warm, with just the perfect amount of lubrication. She rocked her hips sensually and slowly, allowing herself to feel my entire length with each stroke.

We were so wrapped up in each other that it was like we were one. And then I remembered. A lonely day after a week of conferences, too many drinks, and an exotically beautiful woman.

I was about to stop, but then she whispered, "I'm going to come."

And those words unleashed a power in me, urging me to completion. I pumped in and out of her moist pussy and almost fell to my knees when my load exploded inside her. She cried out my name, and I was lost in heavenly bliss.

How could I have possibly forgotten? Worse, how am I going to fix this? What should I do now?

Shame overwhelmed me as I held her while we shuddered from the aftershocks of our passion.

Chapter Nine

NATALIA

We held each other for a while, staying in this moment. I let my breathing calm down. Cassius's heart was pumping fast as his cock softened in my vagina slowly. Instead of a sense of relaxation emanating from him, he seemed suddenly absent or distracted. But I couldn't place my finger on the reason. He almost seemed ashamed, like he was thinking about how he had violated a company policy or something.

Either way, when we lay down to cuddle, I fell asleep in his arms, and I vaguely remember him picking me up from the divan and carrying me to bed. I woke to the sounds of birds and a warm light on my face. I lay there for a while, just breathing in his scent.

But why did he seem so sad and disappointed? Was I not what he wanted?

I tried not to dwell on it and ordered a big breakfast for the two of us for our relaxing time. We quietly sipped our coffees, not bothering with small talk, and awaited breakfast. Cassius curled up again, and I think he fell asleep.

I checked my phone and was startled at how many messages and emails I had. We were making waves in the industry, and all the businesses were noticing it. We were the next big thing in the literary world. My inbox and DM were filled with messages of congratulations and people hinting that they wanted a piece of the action. It felt so satisfying. *So, why did Cassius seem somber?*

I was beginning to feel like it was something I had done. But I couldn't come up with anything when I racked my brain, and I was too pumped up and ready to enter a new stage in my career. I was so proud of myself.

I brought the tray of food to the bed, where Cassius was sleeping, and I started waving bacon under his nose, hoping to entice him into consciousness. He sat up abruptly, and he had the eggs gone in a few seconds, then the toast, saving the bacon for the last bite.

It struck me odd that he ate the same way as me. I was not too fond of mixed food. And I always ate veggies first, then the carbs, and lastly, whatever meat or protein was available. I think I did it to make sure my last bite was the best tasting one.

"Morning," I said once I was sure he was conscious and not on autopilot.

"Good morning, Natalia. Did you sleep well?" he asked, looking like the polite gentleman he could sometimes be.

"I slept fine. The beds and pillows here are amazing."

He nodded and began to get out of the bed. When he stood, I saw that not only was he naked, but he also had morning wood. I stood, walked toward him, and took his firm shaft in my hand.

"Do you need help with this?" I asked coyly.

He raised his eyebrow at me but nodded his assent. I got down on my knees and spat on his erection. Then, using my lips, I spread the lubrication up and down his hard cock. He made a gasping noise and shoved his cock deeper into my mouth. I gagged, producing more saliva. Then, using my fingers as an extension of my mouth, I went slowly up and down his dick.

I drew out my sucks and made a twisting motion with my

hand as I stroked his length. He seemed to like that, judging by how he was panting and making noises of restraint.

"You can cum in my mouth if you want," I said, removing his cock momentarily. I wanted to taste his semen and know that I did a great job pleasing him with my mouth.

He didn't respond, just watched me with those remarkable eyes. I picked up the pace and squeezed his cock harder with my hand, and I could feel his balls tighten as if he may blow his load any second. He dug his hands into my hair and fucked my face. No one had ever done this to me before, and it was oddly liberating. But trying to fit that much of his cock in my mouth stretched my mouth wide.

His hands clenched into fists in my brown locks, and I began to taste semen in my mouth. He pumped it until every drop of semen entered my throat. It was exhilarating. I had never made a man cum before just using my mouth. His whimpers of pleasure slowly died away, and he released the death grip on my hair.

"Sorry," he said.

"Sorry for what?" I was confused about where this was coming from. Cassius wasn't the type to apologize. "Having an intense orgasm is nothing to be sorry about."

"It's not just that. It's everything. From the way I initially treated you to how I just fucked your mouth like you were a toy. It was all disrespectful."

"Did you see me fighting you or telling you to stop?"

"No," he muttered.

"Then quit this whining pretense, and begin acting like the cocky man I know you are."

He raised his eyebrow at me but sighed. "You're right. Like usual."

It was almost time to leave, and we had an excellent scrub-down session in the shower. Cassius was so gentle with me. He washed my genitals, and I returned the favor. He starting to get hard again, and I knew we didn't have time for any more sexual exploits. So I hopped out of the shower and blew out my hair with a dryer.

I then dressed in a sequined green dress that covered me from neck to foot. It hugged tightly to my shape, but no one could dispute it and say the dress was inappropriate, as it left no skin uncovered. But the look in Cassius's eyes made the designer dress worth every penny I spent on it.

I wrapped a faux fox skin around my shoulders and prepared to leave the resort where Cassius and I had grown to care for each other. The driver was ready and took our suitcases. In about an hour, we were on the tarmac about to board the plane.

We sat beside each other, wrapped up in a blanket. After serving us drinks and some snacks, the flight attendant disappeared behind her curtain.

I figured we would start playing around a bit, but instead, we started talking. Well, Cassius began to speak.

"When I was younger, about five or six, I used to dream that I had a different family. My life was nothing like it has been portrayed. I had a pill-addled mother and a father who thought communication was best demonstrated through violence. When I was around, they left me alone for the most part while they attended charity events and art shows. Or they traveled around the world, collecting antiques and attending auctions. They had little time to spare for me, so that's why they shipped me to a boarding school the minute I turned six."

I didn't know why he was sharing all these intimate details with me, but it was an interesting development. I kept quiet, wondering if he would share more.

"The boarding schools they sent me to were filled with other rich brats like me, and they focused primarily on discipline. It was like they were shaping us into soldiers of some sort. I lost count of the number of times I couldn't sit down after one of their punishments. Or they'd crack us over the palms of our hands with a switch. Sometimes the marks were deep enough to draw blood." He held up his palm, and I could see the faint white scars.

"When I told my parents, they said that the school was trying to teach me how to be a man and rule a vast fortune because, eventually, I would have to make my way alone in the world. And the most important thing to learn was that the world was a harsh place that would not care about my feelings. So I began to pay attention to what they were teaching me and tried my best to escape punishment."

He paused for a long while, staring out the window as if the answers to life's secrets were there. "I became cold and calculating. It was a dog-eat-dog world, and I wanted to hold the leash. I became very competitive, ranking at the top of my class in most areas of study. And by the time I left boarding school to head to an Ivy League university, I was already known for my stern reputation and coldheartedness when it came to most areas of my life.

"When I received my trust fund, which was several billion, I began investing in and taking over businesses. I have never had a wife, nor even come close, and I only had one woman stick around long enough to be deemed a girlfriend. Most women left me once they learned that my heart belonged to my money and my professional life and that they were the last priority on my list.

"My childish dream of a family has disappeared. I couldn't imagine having a child now. Not in this godforsaken world. I wouldn't know the first thing about parenting, and I would probably just do what my parents did and let a school raise them."

He drifted off, not making eye contact with me. What he said hurt me, and little did he know, he already had a child. This was the exact reason something had told me to wait and see what would happen naturally instead of presenting Bella to him. If he didn't want a child, that was fine. I would keep Bella for myself.

But why did it hurt so much knowing this about him? Was it because I secretly wanted a family? Did I already love him after so short a period? No, it couldn't be the last one. I didn't believe true love could hit that fast. Infatuation and lust, sure, but in no way was love involved at this point so early in our relationship, or whatever this was.

But a resounding ache settled in my core. I didn't want to poke at it, but I knew the feeling was unwanted. I was really affected by what he said about not wanting children. And I didn't know whether that was for my sake or Bella's. I hoped she never found out about this revelation of her father's. Because if it hurt half as much as the pain I felt now, it would possibly ruin her. No child would want to hear that their parent didn't want them.

But I had to admit that this ache I felt was not merely on her behalf. It was also on mine. *Would he never want a child, even if this relationship thrived and we came to love one another truly? What would happen if I wanted children of my own? Would he never love them and just want to ship them off?* I felt tears start to build.

"Do you have anything to say?" He broke me out of my reverie.

It took me a second to realize he was talking to me and a minute before I figured out the right words to say. "I'm sorry you had to go through all that. I am happy I got to see the relaxed and carefree side of you, even if it was just for one weekend."

"It doesn't have to be just for one weekend," he said, his eyes downcast.

"Are you sure we should be having a relationship while working as partners for the firm?" I asked, genuinely curious.

"It's our business, and as long as we keep things professional in the office, they can't say anything about what we do in our downtime."

"Oh, I guarantee there will be a lot of speculation and gossip."

He waved his hand like he was swatting a bug. "Fuck 'em," he said.

"I'd rather not fuck them," I said with a mischievous grin. I didn't know how I managed to pull off the grin because, deep inside, I was hurting. *Am I falling in love with this sensitive side of him?*

I wasn't sure. All I knew was that I couldn't reveal Bella to him.

The plane landed, and we went our separate ways. We shared a brief kiss before heading in different directions. I jumped into my SUV, and suddenly tears were falling. For a while, I had started to think that I could open up to him about our daughter. But that dream was now thoroughly smashed. I couldn't believe how much it affected me.

I drove home and saw I had a message from Bella's preschool. Worried, I hurriedly dialed the number, and someone answered in a couple of rings. "Tots and Toys Preschool, Mary speaking."

"Hi, Mary, this is Bella's mom, Natalia. Is everything okay?"

"No, we think something is wrong with Bella."

"What do you mean? Has she been hurt?"

"No, it's nothing like that. Bella won't talk anymore or answer questions. She stopped socializing with the other kids and has an almost vacant expression. It's quite unsettling. Has she been acting this way at home?"

"I'm not sure. I have been away from home for a few days. Maybe that's the cause of it."

"Maybe, but in circumstances like these, we suggest you see her general practitioner. They may be able to provide some more insight."

I felt panicky. "I'm coming to pick Bella up right now."

"We will have her ready."

It took mere minutes to get to the preschool, but it felt like hours. When I got there, I dashed to the door. I could see something was wrong with my daughter with one look. She didn't look at me or run to me for a hug like usual. *Did going away for work have something to do with it?* I started blaming myself and went to talk to Bella.

"Is everything okay, Bella?"

She didn't respond.

"Did something happen to you, baby?"

Still no response.

I thanked the day care workers and grabbed Bella's hand, leading her to my vehicle. I strapped her in, talking to her the whole time, but nothing I said got a response. Now my heart was aching for two reasons.

I headed home, scared and feeling lonelier than ever. There was something wrong with my child, and I would get to the bottom of this, one way or another. I pulled into the driveway of our home, and my cell rang. I almost went and answered it, but I had to focus on my child.

I snapped my fingers in her face, but there was only the same vacant look in her eyes, and it was like her soul was gone. In terror for my daughter, I picked her up and carried her inside, desperately wondering what I should do.

Chapter Ten

TINA

I missed Cassius.

It had been about a month since I last saw him, and he was all I could think about. *What was I thinking, cheating on him with Terry?*

I had just wanted to get back at him for ditching me constantly for "work." I hadn't seen him do it or really had any evidence, but I couldn't believe he would work so much. *Wasn't "working late" a euphemism for sleeping with another woman?*

But jealousy raged inside me that he would focus on his business more than me. Sure, I loved the money he provided and the prestige that went with being his girlfriend. But I should have been what he dedicated his time to, not his stinking empire.

That was why, one night, when he stayed late at work, I tried to figure out a way to get back at him, and I soon found myself on Terry's doorstep, standing in the rain. I burst into fake tears when the door opened, and Terry pulled me inside his house. I pulled him in for a hug as I dripped on his hardwood floors, then I started kissing him and tearing at his clothes. At first, he resisted, pulling away and pushing me back. But I started breathing heavily and removing my shirt, and he was gawking at me like a teenager. It was like he had never seen tits before. It was perfect. With a few shed tears, he had fallen into the trap—the loser.

Terry's kisses were so different from Cassius's. They were messy and fueled by lust. A feeling I had seldom got from Cassius. I had tried everything to get him to be more interested in me. When Cassius felt guilty about ignoring me, he would give me his credit card. With it, I bought new perfumes and did my hair and makeup. I spent thousands of dollars on designer clothing to see if any one style of dress or color would catch his eye. But instead of attracting him, I felt as if it was all a wasted effort. It was like the harder I tried, the more distant Cassius became. He probably believed that I was needy. Maybe I was, but it didn't matter. I was fed up with him and his "work."

It took me a few weeks to develop my plan. I would hit Cassius where it hurt him most. And the person that Cassius cared about was Terry, so I'd formulated a plan to sabotage their friendship. It would be simple. I would ruin his friendship with his best friend, Terry Magee, who I would seduce.

At first, whenever I saw Terry, I would play coy or complain about Cassius leaving me alone so much. When really, Cassius had come home duteous every night, just some nights later than others. Then, that night in the rain, my plan had come together.

I had finally convinced Terry that I wanted him, and we had fucked so hard that he'd had me screaming as I came all over his cock. We didn't even make it to the bedroom. With his shining bald head and cerulean-blue eyes, Terry had set me on the kitchen island and went down on me right there beside the spice rack.

I watched as he licked every petal of my nether region. He didn't stop until I was shuddering from an orgasm. I had never been eaten out like that before. It was like he could read every movement of my body. It was deliciously sensual. Then he flipped me over and bit my ass before kissing his way up my spine.

When he entered me, I sighed in relief. It had been so long since I'd felt the heat of a dick inside me. Toys just didn't cut it.

Just like a loveless relationship couldn't. With every stroke of his cock, I couldn't help but smile. With the snap of my fingers, I had ruined their friendship.

Terry pummeled me so hard that the island shook with each thrust. I was gasping for air and quivering because he had turned me on so much. When he reached around with his thick hands and began playing with my clit as he fucked me, I couldn't even stand on my feet anymore. The only thing holding me up was the kitchen island and Terry's girthy, rock-hard staff.

He kissed my shoulder blades and was attentive to every part of my body. And when I came for the third time, he pulled out and sprayed his load all over my back.

Then he instantly regretted it. "What have I done?" he asked himself right in front of me.

My feelings were instantly hurt. I grabbed my panties off the floor where Terry had tossed them and stormed out of his house without a word. He called after me and even chased me to my car, but I slammed the door and squealed my tires as I left his driveway.

That went perfectly, I thought.

Then I began to panic. I knew Terry well enough to know that he would confess everything to Cassius. They had been best friends for ten years, long before I came along. Despite being a big man, I knew he had a soft heart and that a guilty conscience would eat at him. When I got home, I read his texts, and he verified that he would tell Cassius.

He didn't expect it to go well. I knew that this would be the end of my relationship. But at the time, I was more upset that Terry regretted fucking me so fast. I didn't even get the chance to process the event, and there he was telling me that if I didn't say something, he would.

So, I did the only thing I could think of. I disappeared with Cassius's credit card. I went and bought a new car, over $50,000 worth of clothes, makeup, and accessories, and a two-week stay in the Bahamas. Then another week-long all-expenses-paid trip to Mexico.

And I stayed away for three weeks. Cassius had tried to contact me only once, and his email had been crystal clear that he wanted nothing to do with me ever again. I felt like an idiot. He had all the money I needed to live a wealthy life where I wouldn't have to lift a finger. *And what did I get in return?* Nothing. Zip. Zilch.

As time went on, I stopped feeling guilty and instead felt angry. *How dare Cassius break up with me?* For all I knew, he could be sleeping with other women. But I knew he wouldn't. That wasn't in Cassius's "perfect" nature.

That was when I consulted with a lawyer. If I couldn't have Cassius, then I wanted half of everything he owned. I made it my personal mission to ruin him in any way possible.

I started my mission by wooing Terry again.

At first, it didn't work. Terry tried to repair his friendship with Cassius, but he ended up with a broken nose and a restraining order filed against him. He resented me and wouldn't answer my messages for a long while, but I didn't give up. I told him that I'd fallen in love with him over time and wanted to be with him.

But in the beginning, he was suspicious. I eventually wore him down, though, knowing that he was lonely too. He wanted to believe I loved him. And for a while, I even convinced myself that I loved Terry. But then things began to sour. Terry missed Cassius more than he cared about me. And that cut me like a knife. As a result, I wanted them both dead.

I grew bitter when I started losing my court battle with Cassius. Terry openly confessed to the affair, and my fleeing only confirmed it. But Terry thought it would help fix his friendship with his college buddy. Instead, it drove a deeper wedge between them. Cassius never had the restraining order changed, and Terry had refused to see me anymore, calling me names that I should have slapped him for.

I felt lonelier than ever now.

I became obsessed with both Terry and Cassius, and it was like rejection had turned into an aphrodisiac for me. I hired private investigators to look into both of them. I had to find a weakness to exploit. I wanted them both ruined and alone.

Then I discovered there was a woman that Cassius had invited to a romantic resort to meet with another company. I wasn't sure what her role was in the whole situation, but hearing that another woman was with my Cassius made me see red. I wanted the woman dead.

So I got this private investigator to look into Natalia and found out that she had a kid. I paid the investigator handsomely to start a collection of photographs of the child and Natalia's house and the man that lived with her. That way, if she was seeing Cassius, I would have something to threaten her with because there was no way I was going to end this relationship. I would never give up.

The private detective had gotten back to me today, and my worst fears were becoming a reality. The PI had sent me pictures of them getting cozy by a swimming pool and having dinner together. He even let me know that Cassius and this woman had gone into the same room together and hadn't come out until the following day.

Hearing this, I lost my mind, and in a panic, I called the only person I could think of: Terry Magee.

"Hello?" He answered the phone with his gravelly voice.

"Terry, it's Tina."

"I thought I told you to stop contacting me," he said calmly.

"Did you know Cassius is seeing a woman?"

"What? No. Thanks to you, I don't speak to him anymore."

"Thanks to me? It takes two people to fuck, Terry."

"Yes, and I regret it every day. No woman should ever get between best friends. I can't believe I fell for your pathetic ruse. I should have known you were just a lonely little psychopath who only thinks about herself and her twisted desires." His voice dripped venom.

I sputtered, "Y-You fucking hypocrite. You want to get back in his good graces as much as I do, so stop kidding yourself. The way you have been mooning over him seems like he was more to you than just a friend."

"If you are insinuating what I think you are, then this conversation is over. Actually, this is over. Leave me the fuck alone, you cheating whore. Both Cassius and I will do better with you out of our lives. Call me again, and I'll get a restraining order against you."

Then I heard the dial tone.

I sat for a long time, holding the phone in my hand and staring at nothing. I screamed and pelted the phone at the wall. I wanted to tear my hair out. There was nothing I wanted to do more than kill Terry. Not to mention what I wanted to do to that brunette in the pictures. She had nothing on me, and she was practically flat chested like a man.

Realizing I was crying, I wiped the tears away with the back of my hand, leaving a streak of mascara and eyeliner on my skin.

I got up and went to my desk, where I had left the pictures of this woman and her child. Then I looked even closer at the image, and there was something about the child that I couldn't quite put my finger on. Looking from picture to picture, it finally dawned on me. This child looked remarkably like Cassius.

Going through a photo album of Cassius and me, I pulled out a few pictures and compared them. This little girl, who must have been around five years old, resembled Cassius so much that she even had his lopsided grin.

But if Cassius had had a kid, I would have known. *He wouldn't have kept something like this a secret, would he?*

As I held the pictures in my hands, a plan began formulating in my mind.

Things are about to get interesting, I thought, smiling.

NATALIA

It was the next day, and Bella still hadn't spoken a word. She didn't play or color either. Bella just sat, staring off into space like she was contemplating life's mysteries. I tried to get her to play, but she just set the toys aside, even her favorite ones.

After work, I brought her to a child psychologist. The woman had a good reputation and was a leader in the industry. I had read a few of her books about raising a strong child. I liked her way of thinking.

When I arrived at the health clinic, they asked me to stay in the waiting room while the psychologist, Mrs. VanAllen, attempted to interact with Bella. After about a half hour of waiting, they invited me back into the room. I glanced at Bella to see if there was any difference, but she still had that dazed and vacant look in her icy-blue eyes that reminded me so much of her father's.

The psychologist took me into her office, and once we were sitting, she steepled her fingers and leaned against the desk. Her red hair fell in waves down to her shoulders.

"Does she have her father in her life?" she asked outright.

"No," I said honestly, "he doesn't even know she exists." I cast my eyes downward, embarrassed. "He was a one-night stand I had, and we never even exchanged our full names."

The psychologist nodded. "I thought that may be the case." She inhaled deeply before saying, "We see this in children sometimes when they start attending day care or kindergarten. They start hearing about the other children's families, and when they realize that the other kids have fathers in their lives, they clam up. They wonder what is wrong with them and why they have no father. They often put the blame on themselves, primarily due to what another child may have said to them. You know how children can be as vicious as adults sometimes. A child may have said she didn't have a daddy because she was bad or stupid or ugly. Whatever it may be. And the child closes up inside. I think this may have been the case with Bella."

I instantly felt horrified. My baby was like this, and it was all my fault. Tears started leaking out of the corners of my eyes. I quickly wiped them away to prevent my makeup from running.

"How do I fix this?" I asked, hoping for another solution besides telling Cassius the truth.

"Does she have any male role models in her life?" she asked, tapping her fingers on the desk.

"Yes, her uncle Rory. He lives with us, and he's in her daily life."

"I thought maybe introducing her to a male role model might help, but if she already has one, then all I can recommend is therapy. I can visit with her twice a week and try to work with her. I would also recommend that you talk to her day care about possible bullying. It seems like someone hurt her badly to elicit this type of response."

I wondered if it had something to do with me leaving for a few days. I brought it up with the counselor, but she shook her head. "I doubt it has to do with that, but give it a few days. If it was that, then she should perk up again."

"So, in the meantime, what should I do?" I asked, leaning forward and waiting for some solid advice.

"Keep talking and interacting with her as if everything is normal. I would suggest keeping her home for a while. Because if bullying was involved, then seeing the offending child may aggravate the situation." She rested her chin on her steepled fingers.

"I'll take a leave of absence and stay home until she improves," I said softly. I knew I had enough vacation days to stay home for at least a month. Cassius would be able to handle the office. It was probably a good idea that I didn't see him for a while anyway.

"That sounds like the best thing you could do for her," Mrs. VanAllen said with a smile.

It would be so easy if I could open up and tell Cassius about Bella, but after hearing what he had to say about not wanting kids and letting a school raise them, telling him was the last thing I wanted to do. *What was worse, having a coldhearted Dad or an absent one?* It was easier to keep the situation as it had always been.

I thanked the psychologist and gathered Bella and her untouched toys from the floor of the adjacent room. She still wasn't making eye contact, but she clung to me when I picked her up. I brushed her coal-colored hair out of her face and kissed her lightly on the cheek. Another tear fell from my eye.

I strapped Bella into her car seat and took her home, where Rory was waiting to babysit her for the day. I grabbed my laptop and briefcase and headed to work. I gave Bella a kiss and a hug and left with a heavy heart. I wanted her to say "I love you" or anything at all, but she didn't even look at me when I left.

On my way back to work, I was getting out of my black SUV when I felt someone grab the back of my head by my hair and yank me backward. My arms flung out, and I caught the side of the door so I didn't fall to the ground. I whirled around, and reflexively, I slapped out wildly, smacking my attacker across the chest.

A woman with fake thirty-inch-long blond hair stood there, hand on her hip. The woman was totally unfazed by my attempt at self-defense. She was as tall as a model and curled her carefully painted lip in disgust. She shoved what looked like photos into my hands, and I could feel their glossiness.

I looked at one and saw that it was a picture of Bella and me at the park the week before my business trip with Cassius. I flipped it over, and there was another one of Bella and me at the grocery store. In a panic, I flipped through them all. "What are these? Where did you get them?"

"That's my business," she added tartly. "All you need to know is that I can get to you no matter where you go."

I didn't know who this woman was, but I took her seriously. She was clearly unhinged, and I could smell liquor on her.

Then, raising fierce eyes, I glared at the woman. "What do you want?" I snarled. The last thing I wanted to do was show fear to this woman.

"Stay away from Cassius, or both you and the girl will suffer."

"Who are you to tell me who I can and cannot see?" I wondered who this woman was to Cassius. He had told me he didn't have relationships. Maybe she was one of his scorned lovers.

"It doesn't matter who I am. Just know that I am always watching and that your cute little daughter might have a little accident if you do not stay away from Cassius."

"You stay the fuck away from my daughter and me, or I will end you." I pushed her away, and she stumbled in her heels and fell on her ass. I rounded the vehicle and ran to the building's entrance, looking over my shoulder, worried that she would follow me inside.

Once within the safety of the building, I stopped and took a few deep breaths. I was afraid and shaking violently. Not so much for myself but for the sake of my daughter. I had to call the police, get a security system, and immediately take a leave of absence. It was the best way to show the woman I was backing off and avoiding Cassius.

I would do as she asked but not because I was scared of her

threats. Having me followed was crossing a line and then threatening my daughter—unbearable. There was no way I would stand for that, and I would destroy anyone who would dare hurt my child. I wasn't called a business shark for being meek. I decided right then and there that I would start carrying mace. The next time I saw the woman, I would spray first and ask questions later.

That someone was watching Bella and me made me sick to my stomach, my belly was roiling. I would get Rory to keep an eye out for someone watching the house.

I wished so badly that I could confront Cassius and tell him everything. I was so upset my body was vibrating. I wasn't ready to face him and hoped that today would be the day he was too busy to bother me.

I gasped for air in the hallway. My adrenaline and heart rate were high, and I couldn't believe how I had reacted—*pushing a woman and threatening her?* I had never done anything like it.

And how am I going to face Cassius? Hadn't he been opening up to me? The more I thought about it, the more I realized that my body and heart were aching for him. I just wanted to hug him, tell him about his daughter, and pursue this relationship. But after hearing he would send his fictitious child to be raised by a school, there was no way I would ever leave Bella in that sort of environment.

But that wasn't all. Being with Cassius so intimately had definitely changed how I felt about him. Here I was, an executive member of one of the best marketing firms in the US, wishing I could go ask a man to protect me. *Shouldn't I be doing it myself?*

But the way that woman had threatened Bella had drawn out my fangs and claws. What the woman had said had provided me with the perfect excuse to avoid Cassius. I had to admit to myself that I was thankful I had a reason. He had been turning me into a Baxter groupie. The mere thought of his name brought back how it felt to have him penetrating me slowly until I creamed around his cock. It was lust. Because there was no way I was getting feelings for him. It had just been an itch that needed to be scratched. Hard.

But he would not leave my mind. I wanted to make him the answer to all my problems but knew that could never be. I had to admit I was starting to fall for him, despite all the warning signs.

Resolutely, I walked through the central part of the office, heading straight for my desk. I would begin cutting ties immediately, determined to avoid Cassius like his mere presence was poison. It would lead to awkward situations, but I couldn't let this flirtation get in the way of my daughter's well-being.

I sat at my desk and buried my face in my hands. *How am I going to stay away from Cassius?* We were business partners.

I called the board of directors and advised them that I would be using all my banked vacation days for an extended leave of absence. When they inquired why, I simply stated it was a family issue. As I hadn't taken a vacation in the past five years, they didn't push me when I asked for the time off. If they had, I likely would have quit on the spot.

I was going to finish off the day, but that was it. I arranged for all my work to be delivered to my home by courier and advised my secretary as to how to handle conference calls. I would still work remotely when I was really needed, but I would be spending most of my time with Bella.

I found a few security companies and gave them a call. One could be at my home by the time I left the office, so I went with their company. I was not going to sit idly by while someone threatened my family.

Once more, my mind drifted to Cassius. I wondered if he would continue pursuing me or just give up once I was unresponsive. The thought made me feel depressed. He had tons of options for women, and I was sure he would be seeing someone else in a short amount of time.

Well, it had been pleasant while it lasted. But I was more sure than ever that I would cut ties with Cassius for Bella's sake and for my heart, which insisted there was more to it than lust.

Chapter Twelve

CASSIUS

I had loved the brief respite from work. And spending it with one of the most beautiful women I had ever seen was stimulating in more ways than one. I couldn't get over the fact that I had forgotten all about her for the past five years.

I was still wondering how I would let her know that I remembered her without coming right out and saying it. But no idea came to mind. I wished Terry was still around, my former best friend. He had always given excellent advice, but I'd had to draw the line when he slept with Tina, my ex.

He had tried to rekindle our friendship, but I'd gotten a restraining order against him after he'd showed up at my place in an attempt to make things right. Once the trust was broken, I couldn't look at him the same.

I knew that more than likely, Tina was responsible for the affair, but the fact that Terry had given in spoke volumes. Shaking the thoughts of Terry and Tina out of my mind, I found that I couldn't stop thinking of Natalia.

But my cock was causing a significant bulge under my sheets.

I took my cock in my hand and began to stroke slowly while picturing Natalia in her teal bikini with her gorgeous ass and hips bared to the world. I loved how she tasted when I went down on her and the scent that was hers alone, and it reminded me of clean linen and fresh fruit.

I imagined her on her knees before me as I gripped her hair in my hands, her mouth working my cock with her nimble tongue. She was exquisite, and I was now determined to make her mine. I would win her over somehow. I knew she had given her body to me, but now I wanted more than that. I wanted her love.

I was suddenly shocked. *Did I really think that? Do I want her love?*

She was so different from how Tina had been. Tina hadn't listened and bantered with me the way Natalia would. Natalia made me feel warm inside, like a small ember was burning in my chest. Just the thought of her made the ember get warmer. I uncovered my groin and grasped my hard cock in my hand. I was throbbing with need.

I wanted Natalia so bad, and what I had thought had only been lust was changing my whole perspective on women. What I wanted from Natalia was not a few sexual occasions of lust-filled moments. I wanted to be hers. I had never felt that way about a woman before.

I started stroking myself to her smile and the way she had rode me, her small breasts clasped in my palms before I slid my hands down her tiny waist and over those gorgeous hips of hers. I felt the tension in my cock, and I slid my hand harder up and down the shaft. The tension finally rose, and soon I was gasping for air. Natalia was sliding me in and out of her sopping wet pussy, and I remembered how beautiful she was as she rode me. The flush of the skin on her chest was tantalizing. And then, before I knew it, I was splattering semen all over me and the sheets. I wiped it all up with the top sheet and threw it in the laundry hamper. Then I hopped in the hot shower, still quivering from my sexual release.

I got dressed and ready to start another week's work.

Surprisingly, I showed up happy to be back. And as I passed

the employees on my way to my office, I was all smiles and waved to those who waved to me. By the shocked expressions, I knew they thought that my happiness was odd behavior. But it didn't stop me from smiling like a hyena at everyone.

Being around Natalia had done something for me. I felt looser, if that made any sense. I guessed I was not as tense. It had been a wonderful weekend. The sex had been phenomenal, and her company was comforting in its own way. I still wasn't sure what was between us, but I was beginning to feel a bond with her. If this was love, I was beginning to like it.

Entering my office, I threw my briefcase on the desk and took out my laptop. I was ready to start assigning employees to the male magazine project, and I wanted only the best. But looking at the stack of potential employees, I realized I couldn't pick even half of them out. I would have to confer with Natalia. She knew them, and I thought it would be best to leave the decision up to her.

I opened my blinds and saw that my secretary was bustling about. I was secretly waiting to see Natalia head to her corner office so I could pounce on her and give her a private kissing session—and maybe something more.

The thought struck me to buy her a present. I wasn't sure why I thought of that, but I wanted to let her know I appreciated the time we'd spent together.

Finally, I saw her walking through the office. She looked immaculate in a cream-colored sweater and formfitting blue slacks. Her hair was up in a twist, and her lipstick was a bold shade of red. All I could think about was having those red lips around my cock. I was shocked that I was getting hard at the mere sight of her.

That was when doubts began hitting me, and my cock suddenly softened. I was not ready to fall in love. I never wanted that. *What would possess me to desire a woman's love suddenly?* After Tina and Terry, I promised myself I would never trust another woman or person again, and here I was, like a schoolboy, falling for the pretty woman.

But Natalia made me feel different. I wasn't like a mountain she was determined to climb. She saw me as a partner in the business and a partner behind the scenes. Natalia didn't feel the need to spread our entanglements. She was happy just spending time with me. And it didn't seem to me like my feelings were just lust for her too.

I heard a soft rap on the door.

"Enter!" I called.

The door was thick, but my secretary came in with coffee and a stack of papers. "You need to sign all these papers. I went through them and only noted one part I think you'll want your lawyers to look at."

"Thanks," I replied. "I need to discuss a matter with Miss Blake. I will return shortly."

She gave me a knowing and pointed look but nodded, leaving the office. I grabbed the stack of employee files and exited the office. As I walked, I noticed the staff were taking peeks at me, and I just smiled, knowing they were wondering why I was in such a good mood.

I knocked on Natalia's door, and she opened it, looking through the crack of the door.

"Can I help you?" she asked, not inviting me in.

"Um, I wanted to ask for your help concerning the employees."

"What about them?"

"I wanted your insight into which would be best for the newly acquired projects for the men's magazines. Are there any you recommend?"

"Are those the files in your hands?"

I looked down, weirded out by her suddenly cold demeanor. Maybe she was taking being professional at work seriously.

I handed her the files, and she said thanks and closed the door. I stood there in shock for a moment. She basically just blew me off. I walked back to my office in a daze, and I felt a pit form in my gut. That was not the Natalia from the day before. This Natalia was clearly having doubts. That hit me hard. I wanted to give her everything, not just as a business partner, but as her life partner. I was falling in love and now it felt like she was pushing me away.

As I passed my secretary's desk, she reminded me that we had a brainstorming meeting for the new clients in fifteen minutes. I would see Natalia again and figure out what was going on with her, even if that meant pinning her to a wall.

When I entered the meeting room, she wasn't there, which was odd. She was usually at these meetings well ahead of time, setting up visuals and whatnot. The meeting room slowly filled, and then Natalia came in. She was stunning, and she sat in the chair across from me. But when I went to make eye contact with her, she wouldn't look at me.

Natalia looked preoccupied, like she wasn't even paying attention to this meeting, which had been so important to her. She had worked her ass off to attain these clients, and for her to suddenly seem disinterested bothered me.

Something was definitely wrong. I could feel it, but I had no idea what to do about it. Natalia left the meeting hurriedly, and I called after her, but she kept walking as if she didn't hear me. I followed her to her office, and she practically shut the door in my face. Instead of knocking, I opened the door behind her and entered.

"Is everything okay?" I asked her, concerned.

"I am fine," she said, combing a lock of hair away from her face.

I knew when a woman said fine that she was anything but. The stoic look on her face was upsetting me.

"Are we okay?"

She hesitated before nodding. The hesitation made that pit in my stomach grow.

"We're fine, Cassius. I have a lot of work to do. Can we talk later?" I didn't know where the warm and smiling Natalia had gone, but I missed her.

"I wanted to invite you out for dinner sometime this week. Can we set a date?"

She inhaled sharply then fussed with her hair again as locks came out of the twist. "I don't think I have time. I have other things to deal with this week. How about next week or the week after? I'll have to see how my schedule goes, but maybe I can make time. I guess we will see what happens."

I was bewildered. It was almost like nothing had ever happened between this weekend, let alone once before. I abruptly turned away and went back to my office. I had to admit it. Natalia's icy façade had hurt me, and it was like everything we had shared over the weekend had disappeared in a puff of smoke.

She seemed like she almost hated or resented me for some reason. I racked my brain trying to figure out if it was something I said or did, but she was pleasant with me up to the very last second when she hopped into her SUV after our flight back home. This coldness didn't make any sense.

Something must have happened in her personal life. It was the only logical explanation. *But what? Had she been seeing someone else?* Maybe that was it, and they had a falling out over her hooking up with me. That made me angry. It reminded me of Terry and Tina betraying me. If Natalia was seeing another man, she should have told me, not fucked me.

If she had a man, then she really was a she-devil toying with my emotions. Though, typically I didn't have emotions involved when having sex with a woman. In that way, Natalia was turning my world upside down.

Was I actually having an emotional attachment to her? That was very unlike me. I sat down and realized that I was distraught. *How could she show me such a good time and then flip the switch on me?* It was not fair. Then I remembered my father distinctly telling me and beating the thought into my flesh that nothing in life was fair. And as far as I could tell, my father had been right.

But inexplicably, I wanted to go into her office, pick her up, and hold her in my arms. I was also tempted to go and badger her into telling me what was wrong. But neither would work with Natalia, and I knew this as a fact. I would have to wait until she opened up to me again.

I decided right then that I would give her a few days because maybe there was some issue at home she couldn't discuss with me. *Something must have happened, but what?* I was suddenly worried for her and realized I was nervously cracking my knuckles. I hadn't done that in years. It was a nervous habit I'd had when I was younger. I really must love her.

I dove into my work, hoping to distract myself, but after rereading the same page repeatedly, I realized there was no way I would have a productive day. I grabbed my stuff and left the office, still lost in my thoughts. I loved Natalia. *Now, what would I do about it?*

Chapter Thirteen

NATALIA

When Cassius left my office, I turned around, sat down with my back to the door, and let the tears flow. The look of hurt and confusion on his face was heart-wrenching. But I had to keep my distance. I wouldn't dare let that woman hurt Bella.

The back of my head still smarted from where she had yanked on my hair. I had tried to put it up in a twist so no one would notice, but while I was talking to Cassius, strands kept popping out and falling into my face. I pulled out the pins and let my hair fall where it may.

My rejecting Cassius like that had struck me harder than I dared to admit. He had been so happy to see me and had tried to catch my gaze in the meeting a dozen times, but I'd kept my eye on the staff presenting their ideas, even if I didn't pay attention to their words. I would have to review all the briefs later to catch up on what I had missed.

When I caught Cassius not looking at me, I saw a sad tinge to his features. Where before he had appeared happy, now he looked lost, which eerily reminded me of how Bella had been looking since she had fallen silent. She resembled Cassius so much.

When the meeting ended, I shook the hands of the presenters and gave them empty compliments. I felt like a horrible person, but my mind was in self-defense mode, and I couldn't get out of my head. I rushed back to my office, and I could feel Cassius coming up behind me fast.

Cassius practically burst through my door after me. I sat at my desk and faced him down. He asked me if everything was okay, and I lied and said things were fine. I wanted to throw myself into his arms and tell him what that wicked bitch had done and said to me. But I was going to do as she told me and stay away from him. I would not put Bella at risk. Not for anyone.

When he lingered and asked me on a date, I blew him off, and I could see his pained expression as if his stomach had suddenly soured on him. He left my office like a kicked hound. *Would it be wrong to let him hold me just one more time? Shouldn't I tell him about his daughter? Didn't he deserve to know?*

But I didn't know the capabilities of the woman who had attacked me. *If she would do that in broad daylight, what would she do in the dark of night?* She seemed like she had a lot of money, judging by how she was dressed and held herself. People who had money to spare could afford many things, including ways to hurt others if they so desired.

I picked myself up off my office floor and went to my desk, pulling out my makeup bag and attempting to clean up the streaks of makeup that had run down under my chin. My eyes would get puffy from crying, but there wasn't much I could do about that. I reapplied my makeup as best I could. I took my time, losing myself in the simple task. By the time I was done, and the reflection in the mirror looked better, a half hour had passed.

I began packing up boxes of files and briefs to bring home for the next month that I would be away. I called my assistant, Jeremy, and my secretary, Trinda, into my office and let them know how things would be for a while. By the concerned look on Trinda's face, I could tell she wondered what was up. But when she pressed for details, I told her simply that it was a family matter.

I decided to leave the office once I packed up what I needed. Jer and a few other employees helped me lug the boxes of files to my SUV, and I looked around to make sure that the woman was gone. That was when I noticed that Cassius's car was missing from the lot. I knew that I was the cause of his disappearance, and I squeezed my eyes tightly shut to hold back the tears.

"Miss Blake, are you all right?" I felt a warm hand on my shoulder. I guessed I hadn't fooled Jeremy either. I hiccupped when I told him I was okay, and his kind smile warmed me. Leaving the parking lot, I drove home slowly. My eyes were burning from unshed tears, but I knew I had to wait until I got home to let loose and bawl like a baby. The stress from Bella not speaking anymore and rejecting Cassius was almost too much to bear.

I pulled over on the freeway, turning my four-way flashers on. I looked in my rearview mirror for someone following me, but if there was someone, they were good at their job. I felt my phone vibrate and saw that Cassius had texted me.

Natalia,

> *I am not sure what is going on with you, but I want to let you know that you can speak to me about it. I will not judge you. I thought we had a good time, and the way you were acting today worried me. It was like nothing had happened between the two of us. And yes, I remember all those years ago when we had that one-night stand. If I have done anything to offend you, or if you are involved with someone else, just let me know, and I will try to make it right or walk away, depending on what you want. Just know that you have become important to me,*

and I don't want to lose this amazing connection that we have.

Eagerly awaiting your reply,
Cassius

I shoved the phone back into my purse and rested my head on my steering wheel. A knock on my window made me jump and scream. A police officer stood at the window of my SUV.

I rolled down the window. "Yes, Officer?"

"Is everything okay, miss?"

I wiped tears off my face with the back of my hand. "Yes, sir. I was getting emotional and pulled over for safety's sake."

"You don't look like you are okay. Has something happened?"

"As a matter of fact, yes. I was attacked by a woman this morning outside my office. I am not sure who she was, but she threatened my child and me. Is there anything I can do about it?"

"Yes, you can file a report at the police station." He pulled a card with his information on it out of his pocket and handed it to me. "If you have the means, I recommend you get video surveillance and an alarm system for your home to protect your-self. That way, if anything happens, there will be evidence."

"I have already called the security company, I assure you. They can have someone over today."

"I am sorry, my dear. If you file a report, I can have a car watch the neighborhood." He continued, "You can start the process so we can take action next time we get a complaint. I'll follow you until you reach the station and look out for anything suspicious. It's on Munroe Street."

"I know where that is. Thanks a lot."

I sat back in my seat and went faster than was legal all the way to the police station. The police officer stayed with me the entire way. When I parked at the station, I felt a bit conspicuous. The officers that were outside gazed at me with prying eyes. Then the officer that followed me pulled up behind me.

"Driving a little fast, Miss…?"

"Blake. Natalia Blake, to be exact."

"Well, let's get this done, and you can be on your way."

I went inside the station, and the officer introduced himself as Sergeant DeCoste. I gave him a description of the woman, where it occurred, and to whom I suspected she was connected, which was Cassius Baxter. The cop raised an eyebrow at that. He obviously had heard of Cassius before, but he didn't care to enlighten me as to how he knew him.

When we were done, he assured me that there would be a police officer in the neighborhood for the next twenty-four hours and, if I saw anyone, to give him a call right away. I thanked him for his time and hopped back in my SUV. I sped home once I was out of sight of the station.

Soon I was near the safety of my home, I pulled the car into the garage and entered the house through the side entrance.

"Rory, Bella? I am home."

I hoped that Bella would run up to me as she used to, but I did not see or hear her. I heard Rory calling from the kitchen, but I ran into Bella's bedroom instead. When I got there, my heart ached. She was sitting on the floor among her toys but didn't turn to me when I entered.

"Bella, baby girl, it's Mama. Are you okay?"

She didn't answer. I walked over to her, kneeled, and hugged her. She didn't pull away, but I thought she tensed slightly. I felt a painful twinge inside and left before I started to cry.

I walked downstairs and into the kitchen to see Rory putting the finishing touches on our dinner. He was a fantastic cook, which was one of the many reasons I loved having my cousin around. I also wondered why Rory couldn't double as Bella's male role model in her life. But since she hadn't opened up to him, either, it was disconcerting.

I then dove into the tale of the bewigged woman and her threats against Bella and me. Rory disappeared when I said that and came back with a can of mace.

"It's like you're reading my mind, cuz." It had a little belt holster, and I thanked Rory and strapped it on. It looked a bit ridiculous over my work clothes, but I was willing to protect Bella no matter how silly I looked.

"So this woman wants you to stay away from Cassius? Is it safe to say that you two have rekindled some sort of relationship?"

"I don't know," I said hesitantly. "I slept with him during the weekend, and I'm unsure how it happened. I was pretty sure he had no idea we slept together before, but he sent me a message, and it said that he remembered our first time together..." I drifted off, biting my lip.

Cassius had seemed different after we had sex, and he had become more attentive and had even provided some private details of his life that I was sure not every woman he'd banged had gotten to hear.

"You are thinking about a million different things, aren't you?" asked Rory, sprinkling some pepper on his fish.

"No," I said honestly. "I am thinking about him and how it would be so lovely if I could tell him about Bella and have him step up and play the fatherly role she needs."

"I think you should tell him," Rory said bluntly. "First off, he has a right to know, and what he does with that information is totally up to him. Secondly, according to the psychologist, Bella needs her father in her life for whatever reason. Honestly, you already should have told him. God only knows how he will respond if you tell him now, but I think it's time to come clean if you value your friendship and relationship."

I looked at Rory and chewed my mouthful of food. Rory was right, as he often was.

But then the tears started gushing from my eyes. My sinuses filled with fluid, and I was hiccupping. I didn't notice Rory's approach, but his arms snaked around my shoulders, pulling me in tightly. He stroked my hair as if I were a child while I sobbed into his chest. I felt like I was losing my mind.

"Don't worry about that tonight. I think you should go sleep in Bella's room, and I'll stay up and keep guard. With that woman attacking you and with Bella being as she is, I think you need to rest and start fresh. You don't have to tell Cassius immediately. Wait for the opportunity. I'll make you some chamomile tea. Head up to bed. I'll be there in a minute."

He released me, and I got up shakily.

"Don't rush. Take your time. How long did you take off work?"

"A month." My voice quivered.

"Well, chill out. You've done everything you need to do, so now get some rest."

I hugged him again and began making my way upstairs.

When I went into Bella's bedroom, she was sleeping peacefully. I crawled in bed with her, wrapped my arms around her, and prayed that she would start speaking again soon.

Chapter Fourteen

CASSIUS

I heard a knock on my office door. "Come in!" I called. I needed to get an intercom instead of screaming at whoever was behind the door.

In walked Natalia's secretary. I thought her name was Trisha. "Hi, Trisha. How can I help you?"

"It's Trinda, but that's close enough. I was told to inform you that Natalia requested a leave of absence yesterday. She said she has faith that you will be able to manage things in her absence. Miss Blake told me to give these files to you concerning the men's magazine project. They are all the applications for the new positions opening up. She said you gave them to her, but she suggests you hold interviews and pick the candidates yourself based on their eagerness and work history.

"She also told me to tell you that she will be working on some aspects at home, but Miss Blake requests privacy, as she has an emergency family situation." Trinda gave a sharp nod and began walking out of my office.

"Wait, Trinda. How long is her leave of absence?" I was immediately worried.

"Miss Blake said possibly a month or more."

My jaw dropped. The issue must be severe. If I had learned one thing, it was that Natalia was a workaholic. For her to up and take a month off struck me as extremely out of character. Not to mention, the company was on the verge of blowing up in the magazine industry, and I had lost my copilot. I knew I couldn't depend on the rest of the board of directors to assist me. It had to be her.

As Trinda left my office, I picked up my cell phone and dialed Natalia directly. I was immediately sent to her voicemail. The woman had turned off her phone. But I wasn't about to let that sway me from getting in touch with her. I walked purposely out of my office and down to the human resources department.

The intern watching the desk looked terrified of me but pulled herself together.

"I need Miss Blake's home address," I said calmly, though I felt anything but calm.

"Y-Yes, sir," the intern stammered.

I watched her as she wiped sweaty palms on her skirt before entering information into the computer system,

After tapping my foot for about a minute, the sweet-looking intern took out a sticky pad and wrote down Natalia's address. Her hands were shaky as she handed me the note. I hadn't realized how much my cold demeanor affected the staff before. That was something I would have to work on. But not today. Today was all about Natalia and finding out what was wrong.

I thanked the intern and walked away, returning to my office. I opened the door, saw the heap of applications, and decided that I wanted to go figure things out with Natalia right now. I couldn't wait for her to open up to me. I needed to know before I began losing my mind with worry and concern. I had a sneaking suspicion that it had something to do with me, but I still couldn't pinpoint a moment where I felt her feelings for me shift. There had to be more to this leave of absence than I was aware of, and I was about to change that.

I left everything in my office and locked it behind me. I told my secretary that I was going home for the rest of the day and that she should feel free to leave if she didn't have any pressing work.

"We can't all afford to take time off, Mr. Baxter. Would you like me to review the applications and look for outstanding candidates?"

"You'd do that for me?" I was curious as to her reasons why.

"If I run out of other daily tasks, I would gladly take on the job. It also gives me a way to get to know some of my colleagues, their achievements, and their ideas, without having to speak a word to them." She chuckled. "I am an introvert, and warming up to a new staff can be difficult for me. This way, I have insider secrets."

I chuckled along with her. I supposed I was not the only one into spying on people.

I left the office and hopped into my Ferrari. I was happy to discover that Natalia lived in a beautiful part of the city, and I drove cautiously because I knew police officers frequented the area. It took me a while to track down her street in the subdivision, and when I found the place, I was impressed. It looked remarkably like somewhere I would have rented. I wondered if she owned it or was on a lease.

The place had a two-door garage and a loft on the top level of it. The house itself had a wooden exterior that was dark teak. It was a lovely home, nice and large, meant for a family. I pulled into the broad driveway next to her SUV. I looked around at her home, wondering what this said about her personality. All the lawn ornaments were classy, and the various shrubs and flower beds were teeming with life. Either Natalia had a love for gardening, or she hired someone who did.

Then I heard a solid thunk hit my car. I squeezed my eyes together, dreading what I would see. I opened my eyes and saw to the right of me a little girl sitting there, swinging her legs and beaming at me with a crooked smile. I thought it was cute because that was how others described my grin. I smiled back at her and got out of the car, looking for damage and for whatever hit the luxury vehicle.

I caught a softball before it rolled under the car, and I checked for a ding but didn't see one. I sighed in relief. The last thing I wanted to do was repair my vehicle. I didn't trust mechanics with my babies. When I'd had a minor fender bender a year ago, I'd had to go back three times to get the damn thing fixed appropriately.

Holding the ball out to the little girl, I asked, "Is this yours?"

Instead of answering or taking the ball, she spread her arms wide like she wanted to be picked up. She was a tiny thing, with cute rosebud lips that reminded me of Natalia's. I couldn't leave her sitting there when she wanted to be held.

I gently scooped her up, unsure of how to hold her properly. I held her like a baby, which she seemed to like. Her tiny fingers toyed with my ears as her gaze penetrated me. It was like she was already comfortable with me. I noted that something about her eyes looked familiar, but I couldn't figure out what.

Why is this random child so trusting of me? All I knew for sure was that I had never felt so connected to a child before.

"Where's your mommy?" I asked, not really expecting a coherent answer. She was a kid, after all. And by her size, I guessed that she couldn't be much older than two.

"Mommy's inside getting ice cream," she said before sticking a chubby little finger in her mouth. She was so innocent and precious. And that's when I noticed that she had Natalia's chin and coloring.

"What's your name?" I asked, wondering how she was related to Natalia.

The hair and eyes were different, but as I looked at the little girl, I realized how much she did resemble Natalia.

"Bella." She smiled around her finger.

It felt like my heart was melting. I couldn't remember the last time I'd held a child or if I ever had. I'd always felt that children were afraid of me, but this little girl was precious.

"Hi, Bella, my name is Cassius."

I saw her mouthing my name. It wasn't one she had heard before.

"How old are you, Bella?" I looked at her long eyelashes and the rosiness of her cheeks.

"I'm four," she said, holding up her fingers to emphasize her words.

"Wow, you are much older than I thought you were."

Her tiny brows furrowed quizzically. Yep, she was definitely related to Natalia. I had been on the receiving end of those furrowed eyebrows before.

Is she Natalia's child?

"Why are you sitting outside by yourself?" Whoever her mother was, she obviously trusted the neighborhood.

"I like it out here, Cassus." Her mispronunciation of my name was adorable.

I broke out into a grin, and she mimicked me.

"It's Cass-e-us," I corrected her.

She mouthed my name silently again. Watching how her brain worked and her facial expressions as she thought was endearing. If I ever wanted a kid, I hoped she would be like this little angel.

"There is a mean boy at my day care, Cass-e-us."

"What do you mean? Did he hurt you?"

She looked down as if she was embarrassed or wary to say anything. I watched her begin to close up. Bella tensed in my arms, and I was sure she was about to jump out of my grasp and run.

"It's okay. You can tell me. I don't know the kid or the day care. I can be someone you talk to about stuff like that." I gave her a tight squeeze of reassurance as I sat down.

Bella seemed to relax again. She raised a lock of her hair to my head and said, "Hey, Cass-e-us, we have the same color hair."

I looked to see and saw that she was right. Suspicion began to fill me, but I couldn't deal with that now. I wanted to focus all my attention on the friendly child that had taken me in like I was a lost puppy. "So, Bella, what about this mean boy?"

Her face scrunched up like tears were about to be shed.

"It's okay," I said in an attempt to soothe her. I began bouncing her lightly on my knee.

"He said I didn't have a daddy because I was dumb and stinky. And he said that my mother was a whore. I don't know what that is, but he laughed and threw blocks at me, and they hit me in the head."

This was precisely why I hated children. They were as vicious as adults when they wanted to be.

I stroked her jet-black hair and attempted to soothe her with my voice. "I can tell you aren't dumb. And I am holding you, and all I smell is soap and your shampoo. In fact, you smell like cotton candy."

"That's the shampoo I use!" she exclaimed, clapping her hands together in excitement. "You smell good, too, Cass-e-us." She was emphasizing the center of my name too much, but it sounded so cute coming from her lips, and I couldn't muster the courage to tell her differently.

"Thank you, Bella. It's my deodorant and aftershave."

"You smell like a Christmas tree. What's aftershave?"

I couldn't help but chuckle. It was the pine scent of my deodorant. "Aftershave is what a man puts on his face after shaving all the hair off it."

Bella reached her hand up and rubbed my face. "It's so smooth," she said as she rubbed her hand over my chin.

"That's because I shaved this morning. If I didn't, it would be scratchy."

She nodded absentmindedly. I could tell she was processing everything I said. It was a fantastic feeling teaching a child something. Watching as she filed it into her brain was amusing and somehow fulfilling.

I had never felt this feeling before, and it turned my heart to mush. I wondered if it was this way with all young children or just this particular warmhearted child. I hugged her tighter to me and began rocking her slowly. She leaned forward and planted a small kiss on my cheek.

Chapter Fifteen

NATALIA

I heard voices outside and panicked. Someone was out there with my child. I grabbed the ice cream cones without putting the tub back in the freezer and started to rush out. But when I saw through the screen door that it was Cassius, I felt my heart skip a few beats.

I wasn't ready to have this confrontation yet. I should have known Cassius would get my address from HR and seek me out. If anything, he was probably angry with me for taking a leave of absence without consulting with him. It was a crappy thing to have done to him, but my daughter came first. He would have to understand that.

But then there was the second reason he would be upset. He'd probably just learned that I had a child, and he was holding her like she was his own. Cassius would wonder why I hid this fact from him. I realized I was holding my breath and released it in a whoosh.

I didn't move forward and instead watched them interact. Bella had never been open to talking much or cuddling with strangers, but there she was being held like a baby and looking like she enjoyed it. And then I realized something else. *She's talking to Cassius!*

Recognizing this, I wanted to run outside, but I wanted to see how they were getting along. *Why did Bella open up to Cassius? Did she know on some level that this is her father?*

I couldn't hear what they were saying, but I watched her stroke his chin with her fingers. She looked happier and livelier than I had seen her for a while. It looked like her silence had ended too. I watched her face light up at whatever Cassius was saying.

From what he had said on the plane ride, I'd imagined him having an almost cruel demeanor with children. I pictured him being cold and distant, not snuggling up with my Bella the first time he met her. I was shocked.

Then I felt the ice cream dripping down the side of the cone and onto my fingers. I walked to the door.

"Hey," I said through the screen. I couldn't open it with the way they were sitting.

Cassius stood with Bella still in his arms.

"Hi, Mama," Bella said with a big old smile on her face. "Can Cass-e-us have an ice cream too?"

"You're talking again, I see. And yes, if Cassius wants one."

"Sounds delicious," he said as I passed a cone to Bella and proffered the other cone for Cassius. He set Bella back down on the pavement, and she wandered away, focused on her treat.

"How did you get her to talk?" I whispered to Cassius.

"I had no idea she didn't talk. She was like this from the moment I exited the car." He shrugged nonchalantly before taking a lick of the melting ice cream.

"And what are you doing here? I asked for privacy." I was a bit miffed and let him know by my stern expression.

"You will get your privacy from the other employees, but when it comes to me, I must know why and when you will be returning. We're in the middle of a takeover, and you just bailed when we needed you the most." He was clearly upset and not for just disappearing from the company.

"I got you the clients, Cassius. Now it is just a matter of

keeping them by providing them with quality work. You and the rest of the staff can handle it. I did the hard part, and now I need a break for the sake of my daughter."

"You have a family? Why didn't you tell me?"

My mouth dropped open. I didn't know what to say. *How do you tell someone that you didn't think you could trust them fully?* I tried to reassure him. "I promise that we will discuss this later," I said under my breath, glancing at Bella to make sure she could not hear.

When I looked back at Cassius, I could see shell shock written plainly on his face. I could also see the cogs in his brain processing his thoughts.

"I'm going to get an ice cream for myself." I needed the time to separate from him so I could collect myself. *How could one man make my insides churn?* "Bella, I am going to go get ice cream. Are you okay with Cassius?"

"Yes, Mama." And she walked over to Cassius and put her small hand in his. I wondered if this was some genetic instinct that had made them bond so quickly. And I couldn't wait to tell Rory about this whole interaction. I wondered what he would make of it.

I went back inside and quickly filled the cone with ice cream. Then I put the container in the freezer and made my way back outside. I took my time, wondering what I would say to him. *Should I just blurt out that Bella is his?* No, that should wait for a more private setting, where he could react without potentially hurting Bella's feelings.

I was also reeling from his assumption that I had a partner. *What could I tell him to make him go away without alienating him?*

I waited at the screen door for a second. Bella and Cassius were scarfing down their ice creams, and Bella was swinging from his arm like a monkey. I couldn't believe the difference in her.

Opening the screen door made them both look at me.

Cassius's expression was icy, but not when it came to Bella. She was swinging on his arm, and it seemed not to bother him much. He ate his last bite of the cone and swung Bella into his arms again. She giggled. I watched him as he looked at her and could tell they had already formed a bond. It made me happy.

Maybe telling Cassius about her wouldn't be as bad as I had dreaded.

When Cassius looked up at me, his eyes narrowed. I had clearly hurt him by keeping Bella a secret. *How much more hurt would he be when he found out that she was his daughter?* A lump filled my stomach. I shouldn't have kept it from him. But with how he was in the beginning, I couldn't trust him with Bella.

Now that we knew each other better and were amicable and sexually involved again, I should have told him. I felt guilt eating at my core. I had to tell him, and soon.

I sat on the step and began licking at my cone. Cassius's gaze was glued to me, but I pretended not to notice.

"Will you tell me why you need to take a month off work?"

The workaholic in me was already poking at me about missing one day. But Bella came first. I nodded toward Bella while she focused on Cassius. "As I said, it's family business. I will explain further at another time. For now, you need to respect my wishes. Since she seems much better, I could be starting sooner. But I have to see if this is a temporary improvement or not. I'll contact you in a week and let you know more."

He sighed deeply and was clearly disappointed.

I added, "this is not the place or time, Cassius. I promise I will tell you more. I need time."

Bella suddenly chimed in, "Cass-e-us, do you know how to play airplane?"

"I think so." He lifted Bella into the air then started running with her above his head throughout the yard.

She squealed in delight, spreading her arms wide. Cassius was practically glowing. I had never seen him act so carefree. He then helped Bella sit on his shoulders and walked back over to me. I could tell by the look in Bella's eyes that she was happy but was wearing out fast. My baby girl always napped around this time. She rubbed her eyes and let out a yawn.

"Bella?" I questioned, "are you ready for your nap?"

"Yes, Mama," she replied. "Can Cassius tuck me in?"

I looked up into Cassius's ice-colored eyes. *How could he not see how closely she resembles him?* She had his eyes, his hair, and his cleft chin. She would grow up to be gorgeous. And I knew it was due in large part to his genes.

"Ask Cassius," I told her.

Cassius nodded, took her off his shoulders, and held her in both arms like someone would hold a baby. He began rocking her gently. I watched in awe as Bella snuggled her head into his chest, and her eyes began to droop shut. I got up and opened the screen door for them. He didn't move at first and instead watched her as she began dozing off.

The tenderness on his face was touching. He didn't even know Bella was his daughter, and already he was displaying a fatherly nature I hadn't thought he had. He looked up at me, and I could not read the expression on his face. He almost looked confused.

Cassius approached the open door and went through.

I followed him. "Her bedroom is on the second floor. It's the first room on the right." I pointed to the staircase, and he slowly made his way up the stairs. He pushed open the door to her bedroom and looked around. There were a few toys on the floor he had to maneuver around, but soon he was lying her down in the bed. He tucked the pink blanket around her body.

Bella's eyes were closed, and she was already deeply asleep. It was never that easy for me to put her down for a nap. He leaned over and kissed her tenderly on the forehead. "Have a good sleep, Bella." Then he turned around and made his way out of the room.

I went over and kissed Bella too.

But fear suddenly flooded me. I would now have to face

Cassius. I followed him back down to the living room. He went over to a chaise and flopped down on it.

"Why didn't you tell me you had a child?"

So, it would start already.

I didn't know what to say, so I shrugged. "I guess I didn't intend to let you into my personal life. It's not like we were in a relationship or anything. I thought we were just having a good time."

"Are you hiding anything else from me?"

Should I tell him?

Suddenly, I heard a vibration. Cassius reached into his pocket and pulled out his phone. I had been saved in the nick of time.

"For fuck's sake," he said, "they are having a meltdown in the office."

"Do you need—"

He cut me off. "I can handle it. Enjoy your leave of absence." He got up without another word and strode out the door.

I suddenly felt ill and ran to the bathroom and puked up my ice cream. Telling Cassius the truth would be more challenging than I thought. I knew I wasn't ready to face him. But if I didn't tell him soon, I would destroy everything between us. It was then that I realized how much I wanted Cassius in Bella's and my lives. Now, I just had to figure out how to tell him.

Chapter Sixteen

CASSIUS

I left Natalia's place furious with her and with myself. I would save my outburst until Natalia and I had some free and personal time together. She had some serious explaining to do. I felt hurt that she hadn't told me about her family, which may or may not involve another man. And I was confused. Not only had I bonded with her child, but I could actually see myself taking care of Bella in the long run.

But as of now, I didn't know if the child's father was in the picture or even who he might be. I could see that she was deciding how to tell me when I asked, after tucking in Bella, but it seemed hard for her to address the matter. Maybe the father was dead, I surmised. *But if so, why were there men's shoes in the entranceway?*

I could feel my anxiety rising. This turn of events crushed me. And I was disappointed that Natalia didn't feel the same level of trust I'd had with her. I had spilled my guts to her on the plane back from the business trip. Then I paused, realizing why she hadn't opened up to me.

I had been talking to her about my dysfunctional upbringing. And how I didn't believe in family and how I never wanted to be a father. No wonder she turned a cold shoulder toward me. *How am I going to fix this? Do I even want to?*

My feelings toward a family hadn't changed. *Had it?* For some reason, I could not get that angelic child out of my mind. She had been so soft and fragile, and the girl had put her trust in me from the very first second. It was so endearing. I replayed all her innocent gestures and cute mannerisms in my mind and couldn't help but smile.

When I got to the office, I could see that everyone was in a mad scramble. They sounded like a kicked-up hornet's nest. I grabbed the first person I ran into.

"What's going on?" I asked the younger man.

"The head honcho for the fishing magazines is here. He was expecting to meet with someone to discuss the new layout, and no one knows who he's looking for."

I grimaced. "He was supposed to meet with me and whoever I placed in charge of his magazine. I was supposed to select a candidate this morning and have them show me their ideas."

"I have some ideas," he said confidently.

I looked him up and down. "Your name?"

"Robert Hilson." He reached out and gave me a firm handshake.

"Cassius Baxter," I said, returning the gesture. I liked that he knew how to shake hands properly. "Nice to meet you. I'll make the decision in a few minutes. Excuse me," I said and stalked to my office.

My secretary was leafing through file folders and looked up as I approached. "I've narrowed the selection down to five possible candidates. Their ideas stood out from the rest." She handed me five file folders.

"You're a lifesaver!" I exclaimed, grasping her hand and bowing my head in thanks.

My keys jangled as I opened my office, and I sat down quickly and was pleasantly surprised to see that Robert's name was on one of the folders. But I wasn't going to half-ass the decision. I opened it and studied all the images and text. I wanted to bring the candidate with me as I introduced myself.

Robert's ideas were good, but surprisingly, a female angler who had grown up reading this magazine stood out. She seemed to know what the client may be looking for based on what she had read growing up.

I got up from my desk and handed the file folder to my secretary. "This is the one. Bring her right here. She's coming with me to meet... What's his name?"

"Jensen Peters," she said promptly.

"How did I survive without you?" I just didn't know how to show my gratitude, so I offered, "Interested in a raise?"

Her round face smiled warmly as she nodded.

Before I knew it, I was apologizing to the patiently waiting man and presenting Miss Campbell as his project manager. The girl was ecstatic, and as I watched her speak, I could tell she was the right one for the job. Mr. Peters was initially skeptical, but soon they were avidly talking about their love of fishing. Her presentation was on point, and she had won the client's respect by the end of the meeting. I was impressed and was finally able to leave work for the day.

Soon I was on my way home. Then, as I drove, I noticed something odd. A black SUV with darkly tinted windows was following me. The vehicle stood out in my mind for some reason. In fact, I could have sworn I saw the same SUV parked up the road at Natalia's.

I decided to take a circuitous route, and my suspicions were confirmed when I saw him tailing me a few cars back. I stopped and pulled over to the side of the road. I wanted to confront whoever it was, but the SUV drove by me. I couldn't see great through the tinting, but I was sure it was a man I had never seen before.

I started driving again but didn't see the SUV this time. I went home and felt exhausted and emotionally spent. All I wanted to do was fall into bed and sleep the evening away, but I made myself cook up some cod with rice and asparagus for supper. It smelled heavenly, and I gobbled it down in no time.

Then I went to my home gym and pushed myself harder during my routine than I usually did. I was trying not to overthink things about Natalia and Bella. But it seemed the more I tried forcing them out of my mind, the more they popped back in.

There was something entrancing about the two of them. I wanted to go back and see them, but when I checked the clock, it was creeping past eight p.m. Bella would likely be going to sleep soon. I wanted to be angry with Natalia, but I knew it was just because I felt wounded by her silence about her daughter.

Typically when I met people, I heard about their children right away. I had spent the whole weekend with Natalia, and Bella didn't come up once. It didn't make sense.

I shook my head and did another set of sit-ups. Then I sat on the bench and looked at myself in the mirrored wall. *What am I doing?*

I felt so lost my gut ached. *How do I really feel about Natalia and Bella?*

Being with the two of them had felt so completely out of the ordinary. No child had ever been magnetically drawn to me as Bella had been. And holding her in my arms was strangely comforting. I had felt protective, like I'd held her small and precious life in my hands.

I had never even thought of becoming a father. And I hadn't regretted that decision at all. I enjoyed the freedom that being alone bought me. I didn't have to answer to anyone. I was my own boss, and I liked it that way.

But holding Bella and looking at Natalia had made me feel complete in a sense. It was almost like we belonged together.

On the other hand, it also made me afraid. When I looked in the mirror, I could see the fear in my eyes. I turned my head away.

That was a look I hadn't seen on my face since I was a youth. My father and my boarding school had beaten that expression out of me. Or so I'd thought.

Feeling the way I did about Natalia and Bella was a weakness. I was terrified of losing them.

But I shouldn't fear losing them because, as a Baxter, we never lost. But that wasn't true. I had lost Tina to Terry. I had almost lost a client today because I hadn't been able to get Natalia out of my mind.

My professionalism had gone to shit since I'd started falling for Natalia. That was it. There. I was falling for Natalia. Hard.

No woman had ever captivated me as she had. That look of intelligence in those nut-brown doe eyes of hers had me spellbound. And the regal way she held herself oozed confidence. She was exquisite.

My cock stirred in my shorts. I mentally pushed the sexual thoughts away and focused on my main issue. It was Natalia and her lie by omission that bothered me. The fact that she hadn't told me about Bella still bugged me deep down. I was falling for a woman who hadn't trusted me. *Is that because I had to earn her trust? And does she know that I had forgotten about our earlier tryst?*

I suppose if I was in her shoes, I would likely feel the same way. Hurt that I had been forgotten and untrusting because she didn't really know me. And the way I had acted when I'd first started working at the marketing firm probably hadn't helped her form a good image of me. I sighed deeply. *Why am I still so hurt?*

It's because I love her, came the thought, unbidden. And if this was what love was, pining and always wondering, I doubted I wanted any part of it.

But then I remembered her smile as we held hands on the plane. She had no idea how lovely she was. The way her damask cheeks flushed when she was embarrassed brought a smile to my face even now. She was the enchantress, and I was caught up in her magical spell. Then I realized it didn't really matter to me that

Natalia came as a package deal. I wanted her in my life more than anything.

I went into my bedroom, and I collapsed onto the bed. I was sweaty, but I didn't care. I decided I was going to pursue Natalia, whether she had a kid or not. I could see myself taking care of the two of them. I could buy them whatever they wanted and spend as much time with them as I liked. I could truly see us being happy together and becoming a family. I pictured taking them horseback riding and parasailing, and on vacations to my properties around the world.

I wouldn't have to be alone anymore.

My heart swelled at the possibilities, and I drifted off into a deep and peaceful sleep.

Chapter Seventeen

TINA

It was the third time I had heard the same recording, "The number you have dialed is out of service." In a fit of anger, I threw my phone at the wall and screamed. That bastard had changed his number on me. I couldn't believe Cassius had done it.

He still loved me. I knew he did deep down. He couldn't bear to hear my voice anymore. That was it.

I went and retrieved the phone from the floor. I had cracked the screen, but it still worked when I opened it. I called three more times before conceding to the fact that he had changed his number. It didn't necessarily have anything to do with me. I was only calling a couple of times a day and leaving messages.

He was still mine. No matter what happened. I knew he truly loved me. He needed time to forgive me. But he would. It was just a matter of time.

I was debating showing up at his office wearing nothing but a long jacket. *Wouldn't that be a great surprise?* He wouldn't be able to resist. I knew I could do things for him that no other woman could. *I have to do something, but what?*

Maybe hurt that bitch I saw him with, that Natalia Blake and her kid. The woman didn't even have breasts, and her hips were too wide for the rest of her body. *How could he pick that woman when he could have me?*

I walked toward the mirror on the wall and looked at myself. Today I had my usual green contacts in, and I had chosen to wear my auburn wig. My Vera Wang dress hugged my slim physique, and I was well proportioned and tall. I smiled devilishly. My reflection please me.

Pacing back and forth across the room, I began thinking of that whore with Cassius. I dug my fingernails into my palms, barely feeling the pain.

Wondering how I could hurt her had become an obsession for me. I pictured running her over with my car or slipping poison into her food or drink.

And that child that looked so much like Cassius. *Is that his daughter?* It didn't matter. I would hang that girl upside down and whip her until she died from excessive blood loss.

I shocked myself at how deep the loathing had grown within me. I wanted the two of them dead. And I didn't care how it was done, but I wanted slow deaths.

And then I heard the sonorous ding of my doorbell ringing. I walked the distance to the door and opened it.

There stood the man I had tailing Cassius. He was remarkably average looking. It was why I was sure he was the best one to follow Cassius. And so far, he hadn't failed to disappoint me.

"May I come in?" he asked.

"What do you have for me?" I demanded, not stepping aside to let him enter.

He proffered a large manila envelope he held in his hands but didn't pass it to me. "I insist we talk in a more private location."

"Fine," I said, moving to the side and waving him into the entranceway. I closed the heavy door behind him. "So?" I asked, anger seeping into my tone.

He gave me a pointed look before handing me the envelope. He began, "I took multiple photos. Cassius visited this residence in a suburb on the outskirts of town." He handed me a cue card with an address on it.

I didn't recognize the street, but I could search for it on the internet. I had seen images of the woman and her child before. And I had warned that bitch after shoving the pictures into her hands. She should have stayed away from Cassius if she knew what was good for her. But clearly, the woman was stupid.

But as I rifled through the new photos, I felt my heart clench. The first picture was of Cassius getting out of his car. The next was a child reaching out to be held by him. And the next was him cuddling with the little girl. It was the child that looked so like him. *Does he know the child is his now?* The way the two were so familiar with each other led me to believe he knew.

I flipped through the pictures until I saw the bitch coming out of the house carrying ice cream cones. I felt my eyes moisten. That should be me with Cassius's child. *I will kill that woman,* I vowed to myself.

The following picture was zoomed in on that whore. She looked so pleased. I couldn't stand looking at her ugly face, and I ripped the photo in half. She was going to pay for ignoring my threats. "Do you have anything else for me?"

"No. But I saw the three of them enter the house. Cassius didn't stay long, but he carried the child inside. When he came out, he was alone."

"Is there anything else to add?"

"Yes, when I looked into that vacation they took, they were clearly intimate, according to a member of the flight crew."

A low growl escaped my lips. I didn't know what else to say. But I wanted revenge, and I would get it one way or another.

Then the man spoke up. "Will you still be needing my services? I think he caught me tailing him. I will have to rent a new car, but it is still doable."

"Yes," I said huskily over the lump that was suddenly in my throat. I wanted to cry and scream while stabbing that whore. I still couldn't believe she had dared push me to the ground. That had been enough to make me want to kill her. But this. These pictures. Now I wanted to hurt both her and the child more than I wanted to be with Cassius. I would flay the skin off them while he watched.

"Are you able to get me a gun?" I asked bluntly.

The man's eyes widened, but he nodded. "What type of gun?"

"I want one that will splatter someone everywhere," I decided. I tapped my chin thoughtfully. "And do you offer more services?"

"What did you have in mind?" he asked, eyeing me speculatively.

"I think you know."

He tugged on his shirt collar uncomfortably. "Yes, but it is costly."

"Money isn't an issue," I said with a wave of my hand.

"When would you like me to do this task?"

I paused. I wanted to be the one to shoot the bitch in her smarmy face. "Hold off for now. Just keep watching. I want to see how things turn out first. I have an alternate plan I want to attempt first."

"As you wish," he said, bowing.

"You may leave." I opened the door.

He began walking and turned back. "I will report back if anything new occurs."

"Of course you will," I commented before shutting the door in his face. I stalked back to my parlor. I grabbed the phone off the table. It was time to call for some backup.

I had Terry on speed dial, and soon the phone was ringing.

On the third ring, he answered in his deep voice, "Hello?"

"Hi, Terry, it's Tina."

"What do you want?"

I didn't like his tone. "I want Cassius."

"I miss him, too, but we did him dirty, and there is no way he is going to let either of us back into his life."

I didn't like his mindset. Cassius just needed more time, that was all. "Of course, he will. It's just a matter of when. He'll forgive us." I spoke positively, hoping to get his spirits up. "Do you feel guilty about what we did to him?" I queried.

"Always, you made me lose my best friend, Tina." His tone was getting angrier with every word.

"We lost him, Terry. And it should be the two of us who get him back. Help him forgive me. I have a plan." I adjusted my wig in the mirror as I spoke.

"What? No. I am trying to renew my friendship with him on my own. I don't need your help or your schemes." Terry's voice was getting ever more heated.

"Listen to my plan. Cassius is seeing someone, this bitch that I warned to stay away from him. I want to have her and her child taken care of, if you know what I mean. And then he will be hurt and vulnerable, and you can approach him and become friends again. After that, then you can remind him that I am always here for him. I think he would take us both back. What do you think?"

There was a long silence. "Are you fucking serious? Taken care of? What's that supposed to mean?"

"I would think it's obvious," I snarled.

"You're batshit crazy, Tina. I refuse to have any part of this scheme you're working up. That woman and her child haven't done anything, and I will never hurt Cassius in any way ever again. You should be ashamed of yourself."

That wasn't the response I was expecting. "Come on, Terry. Don't you want to be close to Cassius again? This is the best way to do it!"

"My answer is no, Tina. And if you try anything like this, I will tell Cassius. You're fucking nuts. I think you should seriously consider speaking with a psychiatrist and getting yourself a therapist. You are losing touch with reality."

"But he loves me, Terry. I know he does." I pleaded, hoping Terry would agree with me.

"Cassius doesn't love you anymore. I'm not sure he ever did."

I gasped at his statement.

He continued, "Get used to that fact. Cassius will never let you back into his life. I know it, and I am happy to hear he's moved on."

"Say you don't mean it!" I screamed into the phone desperately. "He loved me, and he still does."

"Like I said, Tina, he doesn't. You can't threaten to do away with someone. And if you try to sabotage his relationship, I will contact him and the police. Don't call this number again."

The phone went dead. When I threw it at the wall, I knew it was cracked beyond repair. Terry's rejection was almost as bad as Cassius's.

I walked up to the mirror and punched my reflection. The sound of the mirror cracking satisfied me. I wondered if I hit the whore's face whether it would make a similar sound. I sincerely hoped so. I gazed at my reflection in the cracked mirror. The distortion was oddly fitting.

If Terry wouldn't help, all was not lost. It just meant that I had to take things into my own hands. My first step, destroy Natalia Blake.

Chapter Eighteen

NATALIA

I still couldn't believe that Cassius had been the one to get Bella to speak again. I had expected her to stop talking once she woke up, but when she got out of bed, she was back to being her bubbly self again.

Rory was equally surprised when he returned home from work. Bella had run up and jumped into his arms to give him a hug.

He mouthed to me over her shoulder, "How?"

All I could do was shrug.

The way Cassius had been with her had touched my heart. He was so tender and sweet. After that discussion on the plane, I would have thought he would be cool toward a child, but he'd surprised me.

I was still shocked he had shown up here the way he had. I should have known he would be upset with me for not bothering to explain the reason why I had taken a leave of absence, especially after how intimate we had become.

I was still unsure as to what had triggered Bella's return to normalcy, so I set up an appointment with the psychologist again. I managed to get an appointment for the next day.

Until then, I decided I would enjoy my time with Bella. We played with her dollhouse and made cookies. Then after supper, we cuddled and watched a movie. She fell asleep about halfway through, and instead of taking her to her bed, I tucked her into mine. Then I went downstairs to talk to Rory.

He was making himself a sandwich in the kitchen. When I walked in, he asked, "What changed? Why is she talking again?"

"I have no idea. One minute Bella was sitting on the front step, silent. And then Cassius showed up, and when I came out, she was talking like she had never stopped."

"That's eerie. Do you think Bella somehow knew Cassius is her father?"

"The thought did cross my mind. I'm taking her back to the psychologist tomorrow. Maybe she will have some answers." I reached over and stole a piece of his cheese.

"Well, I hope it's not a temporary thing," Rory stated. "I missed the old Bella. It was nice seeing her acting like a child again. Not the zombie she had become."

"It seemed like Bella was fine until I came back from my trip. Do you think it had to do with me being gone?"

Rory was silently gripping his butter knife. By his posture, I could tell he was trying to figure out what to say. "Yeah, if I could pinpoint anything, I would say it was that."

I knew he was saying it reluctantly, but I felt immediately guilty for being a potential cause of my daughter's strange spell.

I could tell by the look on Rory's face that he felt bad for saying so. He was pointedly not looking at me, focusing on his sandwich like it had the secret to life.

"Have a good night, Rory," I said, my voice wavering. I felt like crying, but didn't want to feel sorry for myself.

I went upstairs and sat on the edge of my bed, gazing at Bella's sleeping form for a while. Tears flowed freely, as I crawled into bed beside her and stroked her hair until I fell asleep.

I was up early the following day and decided to make a big

breakfast for Bella and Rory. But when I went and knocked on Rory's door, I discovered that he was gone. I put a plate in the fridge for him before I took Bella to the psychologist. We followed the same assessment protocol as before. Mrs. VanAllen took Bella into the room and spent time with her. Then she sent Bella to play in the adjoining playroom while discussing the issue with me.

"What has been different in her life since I saw her last?" The psychologist leaned forward and steepled her fingers, elbows resting on her desk.

"Well," I started, "she was still silent up to a day or so ago. And then the guy I am seeing came over. I was inside, getting her and me an ice cream cone, and when I came out, she was sitting in his lap and chatting away like she was completely normal again."

"And this man you are seeing, has she met him before?"

"No, but..." I didn't know how to say this without sounding like an ass. "He's her biological father."

The psychologist's face did not give away a hint of what she was thinking. She remained silent, waiting for me to elaborate.

"He didn't come back into my life until recently. He's actually my coworker at the marketing firm now. He owns the majority share of the company. I didn't tell him that he was her father. He still doesn't know. But they were acting like he had raised her from day one."

She sat pensively for a few moments before saying, "Are you planning on speaking with him about him being her father?"

I looked down at my hands. "I have been afraid to. I don't want Cassius to be angry at me for keeping this a secret from him."

"He deserves to know." She spoke quietly but with an edge to it. "And your daughter deserves to have a father in her life. How was he with her?"

"Gentle. Tender. I had never seen Cassius like that before." I felt my cheeks redden. I tried to explain myself. "I didn't tell him right away because of his mannerisms with people at work. He was cold and uncaring. Rude to everyone, including me. He didn't even remember me. I know I was just a fling to him, but it hurt anyway."

The psychologist nodded sagely. "Understandable. But that is no excuse for not letting him know."

I felt sufficiently reprimanded. I couldn't bring myself to make eye contact with her. "So, what do you think about the situation?"

She paused as if carefully selecting her words. "I believe that on a level, they felt comfortable with each other at the moment."

"Is it possible they knew they're related?" I didn't expect a straight answer from her.

"Anything is possible. But probable..." She trailed off. "As I said, I think they had an instant connection. It happens sometimes. I wouldn't look too much further into it." I was still wondering when she said, "I think they found true comfort with each other. If he is what triggered her into speaking again, then I think that bond needs to be fostered. I cannot tell you what to do, but I recommend helping her strengthen that bond after you tell the father about her. It is best for her mental health and for what I believe would be a mutual benefit for the father and her. Especially if you believe he seemed cold before. This fatherly connection may be the thing that warms him up."

"He has been warming up. To me." My cheeks reddened again. "Well, until we came back from our trip. I have been so focused on Bella that I pushed him aside. And when he showed up, I wasn't expecting that. And now, I just don't know the right way to tell him."

She leaned back into her chair. "Would you like to know my opinion?"

I nodded.

"Call him and tell him as soon as possible. Every day you wait will make things worse when you do tell him. Explain yourself, and be ready for his reaction, whatever it may be. And give him time to process things. Put your daughter and his relationship before yours and his. See what happens from there."

I felt chastened. I should have opened up to Cassius sooner. I knew that.

She began speaking again. "As for your daughter, don't give her time to feel alone or sad. Play with her, and involve her in the most mundane activities. Like getting a small broom so she can help you sweep or a cloth to help wipe things down. Children benefit from a routine, so begin to wake her at the same time and put her to sleep at the same time. Bathe her at the same time of day. Eat regular meals, and take her outdoors for walks and to play at parks."

I took everything in. I had always done things like this with Bella. But I supposed I had relied on Rory to handle a large share of the responsibilities. Since I was taking time off work, I could definitely improve her schedule. I started making plans in my head to create a weekly schedule of activities and chores she could help me with.

"Are you going to take my advice?" the psychologist asked with piercing eyes.

"Yes, of course. I will contact the father soon and start keeping a strict schedule for Bella. I have taken over a month off work to help her. Do you think a vacation or something would be good? Maybe taking her out of the environment may help."

Mrs.VanAllen shook her head. "For now, keep her on a schedule at home. And if she is still showing improvement in a few weeks, we will discuss the opportunity of a short vacation with her."

"Okay," I said. "Do you have any other advice you wish to share?"

"I think you have a difficult decision to make and carry out. Try to keep your head above water. He may turn hostile against you and bring you to court for the sake of the child. Hopefully, between the two of you, you can make a decision together and then mediate the situation without getting a judge involved."

"I am hoping for more than that," I confided. "I want the three of us to become a family."

"Don't weigh all your hopes and dreams on that outcome. You do not know how Bella's father will react."

I could hear the unspoken doubt. "I won't," I reassured her. "I'd be furious with myself if I were in his shoes. I am expecting the worst but hoping for the best."

"That's the best way to view the situation. Our time is almost up. Was there anything else you'd like to discuss?"

I shook my head. "No, I know what I have to do."

"Don't beat yourself up too badly, and remember to encourage the relationship with the father. Take her to see him often once all the dust settles."

"Thank you for your time, Mrs. VanAllen. I appreciate it."

She graciously showed me out of the office, and I collected Bella from the playroom. She was playing with a child's kitchen set and had set up some stuffed toys at a play table. I loved the difference that I could see in her already.

When I got home, Rory was in the kitchen as always, making what looked like a large lunch. "Thanks for breakfast," he said.

"It's the least I could do." I then focused the conversation on Bella. "The psychologist advised me to tell Cassius as soon as possible and that I should let them spend time together. But no matter how it is, I still feel conflicted. I am happy she formed a bond with him. But I'm worried he will be angry with me beyond repair."

Rory inhaled deeply. "I am glad the psychologist told you that, like I had before. Maybe now you will listen. Bella deserves to have a father, and you deserve to be happy. But the longer you wait, the harder it will be for Cassius not to think of you as a liar and a coward."

"Could you be any blunter?" I asked, flinching.

"I'm just being honest."

I scowled at him, but he was right. It was time I faced the music.

"Get Bella, and let's have some lunch together." He smiled gently.

I called Bella, and she came tearing into the kitchen wearing a pink tutu and cuddling her bear.

I picked her up. "No running in the kitchen, Bella."

"Sorry, Mama." She puckered up and laid a sloppy kiss on my cheek.

I had my baby back. Now it was time to tell Cassius.

God, please let him accept us both.

Chapter Nineteen

CASSIUS

I was working my ass off on a brief for the erotic male magazine's new branding. It was intensive work. Everything had to be on point. I couldn't afford to take much of a break, even though it was almost eight p.m.

With Natalia gone, much of what she was supposed to handle fell on me. Not only did I have to delegate work, but I also had to oversee the projects and briefs, plus negotiate and present the individual projects.

Luckily, I had a lot of help, and Vera was a godsend. I asked her if she needed any extra hands and then got Robert Hilson, the spunky kid who had introduced himself to me the other day, to help her as her runner. I also gave them both a raise. Without them, the loss of Natalia would have destroyed the relationships with our new clients.

I was stressed beyond belief and had been working on this one brief since I'd started at seven this morning. It was almost ready for printing. The layout looked perfect. I had met all the magazine's specifications, and all I needed to do was run it by the team in charge of the magazine in the morning. The presentation was set for the following afternoon.

I felt relieved, and when I looked up from my desk, the office was a ghost town. I hadn't even noticed anyone leaving.

Standing, I stretched sore and unworked muscles, trying to wake myself a bit before driving home. I turned to gaze at the city. It seemed so small from up here.

Then I heard my phone vibrating on the desk. I hoped it was Natalia. I rushed to the phone and saw that it was an unknown number. It piqued my curiosity, and I answered it, praying it wasn't another call from Tina.

"Hello?"

"Hey."

I recognized the voice instantly. "Terry, how did you get this number?" I had changed it after the drama with Tina. Switching all my contacts to the new number had been a hassle. I was displeased that Terry had found my new number so quickly.

"I have my ways," he said evasively.

"Well, please lose the number. I don't want to speak with you ever again."

"Wait!" he hollered as I pressed the end call button.

I tossed the phone down on the desk. When it rang again, I just ignored it. But Terry was like a dog with a bone when he wanted something.

After the tenth call, I picked it up. "You know, I have a restraining order against you for a reason. There is nothing you can do or say that could possibly interest me."

"Listen, please." He was using his manners, which shocked me. "I know I fucked up. I don't expect you to forgive me. I hope that someday we can be friends again, but that is not why I am calling."

"Okay," I said, "then, why are you calling?"

"It's because of Tina." He paused.

"I don't want to hear anything about that stupid, cheating cunt. Don't you dare try to help Tina weasel back into my life. I changed my number for a reason. That bitch wouldn't stop calling me all day long, every day." My tone was heated.

"She's planning on doing something, Cassius." He spoke seriously. "I don't know what, but she told me she wants to do away with the woman you are seeing and hurt her child."

My anger was now red-hot. I clenched my fist. "Do away with? What is that supposed to mean?"

"Tina has lost her mind, Cassius. She still believes you love her and that it's only a matter of time until you take her back." He continued, "And she said that she wants you vulnerable. Like you would be after she gets rid of them."

I started thinking of the SUV that had been trailing me. *Was Tina responsible for that?* "Terry, is she following me?" I demanded.

"I wouldn't know, but it sounds like she is. She knows you're seeing someone new. She said that she warned the woman to stay away from you. She's off her rocker. I told her never to contact me again. She thought I would cooperate with her little charade, but I told Tina I would never do anything to hurt you ever again," he ended, sounding passive and apologetic. "I mean it, Cassius. I will always be here if you need a friend."

"I thought that was the case, but friends don't sleep with each other's women."

"I know, and I take full responsibility, but Tina was using me to get you to pay more attention to her. I even told her that I doubted you ever truly loved her, hoping that would deter her from acting on anything. But I don't think I got through to her. I think she was expecting a different outcome. And her plan seemed well fleshed out. That's why I am calling. To give you advanced warning so you can protect your new woman and her child as well as yourself."

I paused. I wondered if I dared to let Terry into my life again. I missed our bond and the way we would talk to each other. I had been more hurt that Terry had done that to me than I had been over the loss of Tina. So maybe Terry was right; I never truly loved her.

But no. It still didn't make the betrayal okay, and I couldn't bring myself to forgive Terry.

"I appreciate the heads up. But this doesn't change things between us. You destroyed our friendship. And there is nothing you can do or say to change it. I am sorry." Then I swiftly hung up.

So, Tina was plotting something, something that Terry was worried about enough to call me. I would need a protection unit for Natalia, Bella, and myself. And I would watch out for anyone tailing me again on the way home.

I put my computer in its bag and gathered my things. Knowing that Tina could be doing anything made me paranoid. I called a security company.

"Hi, this is Cassius Baxter. I am looking for two units. One would need to be discreet. I don't want the people under their protection to know about their presence. And I want one for myself. I don't care about the costs, and this should be effective immediately."

"What individuals are they supposed to protect these people against?"

"My ex and anyone she would hire to tail us or harm us. I want a four-person team sent to this address." I gave the woman the address and described Natalia and Bella. I also let her know that another man may be living in the same home. It still irked me that I didn't know who he was.

"For me, I need three guards—one as an escort and two to keep their distance but watch my surroundings like my office and home. Can you do all this immediately?"

"Once the deposit is paid, we will send the requested teams."

I gave her my credit card and paid for a week's security in one go. I couldn't be too careful. Tina was a snake and one that needed her head cut off.

"Have them meet me at my house. I am heading there now."

I left my office, got into my speed demon, and drove home above the speed limit. I didn't see any cars following me. I figured they would have ditched the SUV, but as I was speeding, I doubted they would have a vehicle that could keep up.

I left my baby in the driveway of my home and rushed inside. I checked my cameras for any potential spies, thieves, or worse, but all the feeds came up empty for the past twenty-four hours. Satisfied, I went to the kitchen.

Then there was a knock on the door. I opened it to see a small Asian man in a suit. "Mr. Baxter," he greeted me with a bow. "I am your security detail for the night. My associates are guarding the perimeter of your home. Would you like me to search the premises and all entry points?"

"Yes, please, Mr....?"

"Lee, sir."

"Mr. Lee."

"No, it's just Lee, Mr. Baxter. I'll be about my duties now."

I nodded and went back to the kitchen. I was famished and needed to eat something before working out. I also needed to call Natalia. I had to hear her voice and know she was okay, and I wanted to invite her out for dinner. I wanted to talk to her about how I remembered her, after I had dropped that bomb in my text. She likely thought I was an ass already, unless she had forgotten about me. I hoped that was the case.

I pulled out a container of chicken salad and ate quickly. I saw Lee enter the kitchen and check the window.

"Mr. Baxter, I recommend updating the locks on your windows. Most can be slipped with a knife. And I believe you should set up spotlights when your cameras detect humans or motion. There are newer solar-powered cameras that I can get dispatch to order for you, and the company will also install everything. The doors are all solid, so nothing to worry about there. But these are my recommendations."

"Set it up, and charge it to my account."

Lee nodded and picked up his cell phone as he walked into another room.

After the last bite and a drink of chamomile tea, I grabbed my phone and dialed Natalia.

"Hello?" Her voice was like smoke and pepper. I loved the sound.

"Hi, Natalia. It's Cassius. How are you doing?"

"Great. I wanted to call you. We have something we need to discuss." Her voice wavered on the last word.

It made me uneasy, and my muscles tensed as sweat started seeping through my skin. "What is it?" I asked, worried.

"It's something best discussed in person. It's too important for a simple phone call."

Now my palms were sweating. The last thing I wanted was more conflict between us. Keeping Bella a secret from me was hard enough for me to deal with. It made me feel like she didn't trust me, which affected me more than it usually would. I wasn't just loving and leaving her. I wanted more from her.

"Can you please tell me," I begged. "The wondering is driving me insane."

"No, Cassius. Can we meet somewhere soon?" Her voice was hushed.

"I'll take you to dinner tomorrow night. We can rent out a private dining room. That will give us all the privacy we need. Can you tell me if it is something I need to worry about?"

"I don't know how you will take it. But it's important. That's all I can say about it for now."

"Fine." I felt upset and queasy. *How could this woman evoke so many feelings in me?* I had never been like this with any other woman. My guts twisted, and I felt like I would throw up.

"Cassius, where would you like to meet?"

I gave her the restaurant's name and address and asked, "Will I be upset?"

"More than likely," she said so quietly I had to strain to hear her.

"Okay," I said, forcing a smile. "I look forward to discussing matters with you tomorrow. Have a goodnight, Miss Blake." Then I hung up.

It was a cruel way to end the conversation so formally, but I couldn't stand to speak another word to her. I had a feeling she was going to dump something huge on me, like she had a husband, even though Natalia claimed she was single.

I walked to my bedroom and plopped down on the bed—screw working out. I needed the oblivion of sleep. I pulled the blankets over my clothes and nodded off in minutes. And my last thought was, *Is Natalia Blake worth this stress?* For that, I had no answer.

Chapter Twenty

NATALIA

I got ready early. Cassius was going to send his driver over for me. I wondered about that, worried that if he didn't like what I had to say or got mad at me that I would be stranded, but I decided it was a risk I would have to take. When the car pulled up, I noticed the driver was new. He was a slight Asian fellow with a serious demeanor.

I thanked him graciously as he opened the door. He simply bowed and climbed back into the driver's seat. I slid in next to Cassius. My first reaction was to pull him in close and passionately kiss him, but tonight wasn't about pleasure. It was time to face the music and tell him the truth.

The fact that I had been avoiding him seemed like it had created a vast gulf between us, and I was worried that it would only get larger. We even kept the distance between us as we sat in the back of the town car.

Up and leaving him at work had not worked out in my favor. And it seemed he was still upset that I didn't even tell him I had a daughter. Now I was imagining what it would be like when he realized I didn't just hide the fact that I had a daughter but I was hiding the fact that said daughter was his.

By the end of the night, he might never want to see me again.

Or worse, he might try to take my daughter away. He had the money and influence. He could do it if he wanted. I silently prayed that it wouldn't come to that.

He took my hand. "Whatever it is, it can't be all that bad." He continued, "And there is something I want to talk about first. Should we do this before or after our meal?"

"Honestly," I said, "I just don't know." I bit my lip, unsure if I should spill the beans now or wait until we were trapped in the private dining room. "I don't know if I can eat at all. My stomach is roiling."

He rested a hand on my cheek and rubbed his thumb gently across it. "Don't be afraid. Nothing you say could ruin how I feel about you. I am disappointed that you kept things from me, especially something as crucial to your life as a child."

A tear dripped out of the corner of my eye, and he wiped it away with his thumb.

I was ready to tell him right then and there, but I didn't want this tender moment to end. This man had more layers to him than an onion. *Why am I still doubting him?*

I pulled away. I didn't deserve the tiny bit of comfort Cassius was trying to give me.

He had opened up to me on the trip, especially on the plane ride. *And what did I do?* I ran and hid. I was hiding behind my daughter's mental affliction so that I had an excuse to keep myself away from him and a reason to keep his daughter hidden.

But what he had said about never wanting children had affected me more than I would like to admit. I wanted him to become part of the family, and he didn't want one.

Rory was right. I knew what I wanted, but I couldn't be honest enough with either Cassius or myself because I was afraid of rejection. And now that I had waited so long, I wasn't sure if he would ever trust me again.

"Why are you tensing up?"

His voice jolted me from my meanderings. I stuttered, not knowing how to communicate how I felt at that moment. "I'm s-s-sorry. I am just nervous."

I felt the movement of the car as it parked, and the Asian man opened the door for us, offering me a hand as I climbed out. My gold-and-forest-green satin dress glimmered as I straightened it.

Cassius, in a black tuxedo, slid out behind me and offered me his arm. I laid my hand delicately in the crook of his elbow and let him guide me inside. Men were opening the heavy wooden doors for the guests, and the door led to a massive entryway with staircases on both sides. A heavy crystal chandelier lit up the room.

A beautiful hostess with white-blond hair in a twist and a silver dress walked up to greet us. "Your name, sir?" She spoke with a heavy Russian accent.

"Baxter," he replied.

The woman's eyes lit up. She gave me a once-over and clearly found me wanting. All her attention was on Cassius after that. The woman spoke to him as if I weren't even there. "We have your private dining room. Please follow me, Mr. Baxter."

She purposely sashayed her hips as she walked ahead, making her ass sway hypnotically. But when I peeked to see if Cassius was staring at her, I was surprised to see him looking at me with a gentle smile on his face.

I knew he wouldn't be smiling for long, but I took the time to appreciate this moment. I was so sure it would be the last smile shared between us.

We entered a room with green walls and a rich-brown hardwood floor. The heavy dark wooden table was set for two-place seatings. They weren't across the wide table but positioned side by side.

Cassius pulled out a chair, and I sat down, thanking him.

He then took the seat beside me and looked at the hostess. "What are the specials for the evening?"

"Surf and turf and cedar-smoked salmon and pilaf. I will send a waitress in to take your order." She spun on her heels and walked out the door, head held high.

"I don't think hostesses like taking orders," he commented. "That's why I make it a point to ask them." He chuckled at his audacity.

I just shook my head.

"If there is spit in our meals, at least we know why," I said, pushing on his shoulder gently. He gave me that lopsided grin, and all I could see was Bella.

I looked down at my hands in my lap. Then Cassius reached over and took one in his hand. He kissed the back of my fingers gently.

"I wanted to talk about something. How I remember you from that night long ago. I remembered the way you smelled and the eroticism of the night. I didn't know how to tell you without offending you."

The first thing I wanted to ask was why he didn't tell me earlier, but I knew that it would be hypocritical if I said that. Instead, I remained silent, hoping that Cassius would fill the quiet.

"I am sorry I didn't tell you sooner. I realized who you were on the trip when we were making love. I was used to doing the love-them-and-leave-them thing at that point in my life. I never thought I would see you again, even though you gave me an unforgettable night. I just wanted to apologize."

That made me feel even worse about myself. Forgetting me was something forgivable. Keeping Cassius's child from him was a whole new level of shame.

The waiter entered, bringing in a plate of fresh garlic bread and Caesar salad. He then took our orders, and we both chose the surf and turf. It had been so long since I'd had a good steak-and-lobster feed.

"Perfect," Cassius said. "I'm starving." He dished up a plate for both of us.

I picked at the salad, and the warm bread went into my tummy, saving it from the urge to vomit.

We set aside our plates when we had our fill, and Cassius turned to me.

"Now," he said, "will you tell me who the man is that lives with you?" His voice sounded choked, and his eyes narrowed in suspicion.

I exhaled deeply and was a bit relieved. "That's my cousin, Rory. He has been helping out Bella and me since she was born. He lives in the in-law suite above the garage of my house. He makes meals and takes Bella to day care. I don't know how I would have survived without him."

His eyes relaxed, and he squeezed my hand. "Then I am happy that things have worked out for you two."

"Yes, I'm thankful," I said, smiling slightly and looking at my small hand in his larger one.

When I looked back up at his face, he had a serious look. "Is there something you still need to tell me?"

I paused, removed my hand from his, and sat up straighter. Looking back at him, I said, "Bella is your child, Cassius. After that night we had together, I got pregnant. I didn't know how to get in touch with you, so I raised her with the help of Rory."

Cassius's face reddened, but I could not read which of his feelings were dominant. *Is he angry?*

"She has your hair and eyes. I am surprised you didn't notice that. She's four years old and even has your grin." I paused, trying to gauge his reaction. I still couldn't read him. His face had a severe cast to it.

He coughed, then said quietly, "I have a daughter? And it is your charming daughter, Bella?"

I watched as a smile suffused his face.

"There was something about her. I wanted to hold her and play with her longer the other day. She seemed so cute and innocent."

"She is cute and innocent," I pointed out. "I'm sorry I never told you. I had my reasons."

"I have been back in your life for a few weeks. Why didn't you tell me sooner?" His voice slowly got softer as he spoke. "You could have told me on the business trip. Or the day I tucked her into bed. I'm disappointed and do not understand how you could keep this from me."

I sat there looking at my hands again. Then I lifted my head and looked him boldly in the eyes. "You were mean when you first got here. You didn't give a damn about our staff. You were rude to me, and just all-around ignorant. I recognized you from the get-go, and you didn't even take the time to really look at me."

I stopped and realized I was glaring at him. "I didn't want to bring you into Bella's life because I thought you would be an asshole, in and out of her life and hard to deal with. I didn't want that for my baby girl."

Continuing, I said, "It wasn't until the trip when I let my guard down. I realized you were more than I had initially thought you were. But then, when you told me you didn't want children and would let a school raise them, I knew right then that I should just let things be. So I avoided you."

Tears were flowing freely down my cheeks. "And then Bella stopped talking until you showed up on my doorstep. And I realized that maybe you were what she needed. But I still spoke with Bella's psychologist, who said it was fatherly love that Bella was likely missing. And when Bella trusted you from the start and let you hold her and comfort her, I knew it was time to tell you. I am sorry that it took so long. But do you blame me?"

He ran his fingers through his hair and tore his hurt-filled eyes away from mine. A knock on the door announced the server with our meals.

As the server pushed the tray in, Cassius turned to him and said, "Thank you. We will serve ourselves." He handed the server a tip and grabbed the plates and the heated pots of garlic butter.

"No need to be wasting a delicious meal. We can be civil about this, especially for Bella's sake. But I will not hide that I am disappointed and hurt by your choices." Then he turned back to me. "I can't believe you thought I wouldn't stand up to my duties as a father. I'm not a monster, Natalia. I take care of my own."

"I—" I started to say that I knew that, but he cut me off.

"And I can't believe that you slept with me not once but multiple times and that you still didn't trust me."

I flushed in shame and looked down at my hands again. "When you put it that way, you make me feel like I treated you cheaply and unfairly. I just wanted to build something between us so that the transition for bringing Bella into your life would go smoother because we had been together intimately. I thought it might help. I'm sorry."

He was cutting at his steak and took a bite, chewing it thoroughly while he searched for what he was going to say next. "I think what hurts me the most right now is that you didn't believe my affection." He set down his fork and knife and cleared his throat. "No, it isn't plain old affection to me. It's love. And my love for you was genuine. Can't you tell how I feel about you? You are like fire in my veins, and all that kept me going was believing that you felt the same. But knowing all of this now and learning that I was not worthy of your trust or to even be in our daughter's life has hurt me severely... I'm not angry. I don't know how to feel. But disappointment is definitely in the mix." He pushed his chair away from the table and stood. His stance was rigid, and his face expressionless.

I reached out a hand and touched the sleeve of his arm. He didn't pull away, nor did he hold still. He took a step back, and I instantly felt his rejection.

I blurted out, "I'm sorry, Cassius. I was doing what I thought was best for Bella. And I stand by that decision. Can you blame me? I didn't know if you were just going to 'love me and leave me' or if you were really falling for me. And after what you said about children, I was scared you'd take her away and shove her in some boarding school. That's not the life I want for my child or me. But I want you to forgive me. I want us to be more."

"I don't know what I want anymore." His ice-blue eyes had a sheen of tears as they met my brown ones. I saw real hurt there now. "I can't eat. I'm sorry, Natalia. I cannot stay." He used a napkin and wiped his eyes. The tears in his eyes had begun to fall, and he turned away from me to hide them.

His voice was choked as he said, "I need some time, Natalia. Please respect that and do not contact me. I will be in touch when I am ready. Enjoy your time off with Bella. I'll have Lee drive you home."

He turned and walked away. At the closing of the door, I put my face in my hands and began sobbing. I had done it. I had told him the truth. And now I may have lost him forever. Lies, even lies by omission, could ruin everything. Rory had been right. I should have told him the minute he was back in my life. He had a right to know, no matter how I felt about him. And just because I'd wanted him to feel and act a certain way was not a good enough excuse to keep it from him.

He would never trust me now. He would always wonder if there was something else I was hiding. I knew that was how I would feel. *Could we surmount this problem?* I didn't know.

A knock on the door sounded, and I hastily wiped my eye makeup that I knew must be dripping down my face. "Come in."

Our server entered with a concerned look on his face. "Was something wrong with the meal?"

I shook my head but couldn't speak around the lump in my throat.

The Asian man that had been driving the car followed the youth in and handed the server a hundred-dollar bill. "Please bag these meals up," he said with a heavy accent.

In a few minutes, the server returned with a paper bag.

"Follow me, Miss Blake," Lee said, picking up the bag. "I will see you safely to your home."

I made sure I grabbed my purse and left, following the scent of steaks and lobster that I no longer had any desire to eat. When I slid into the car, I hoped Cassius would be there, but he was not. The tears started again, and I let out little hiccupping sobs. I had ruined everything. And I had no one to blame but myself.

Chapter Twenty-One

CASSIUS

I was a father. I was a father of a beautiful and charming little girl that had captured my heart with just one meeting.

I thought that maybe on some level, I instinctively had known she was mine. And when Natalia had pointed out that Bella and I shared the same eye and hair color, as well as the grin, I couldn't believe I had missed it.

Here I was worried about having to compete with Bella's father, and it was me the whole time. And I had missed so much, like her first word, her first step, even her birth. That was four years I would never get back, and the worst part was that I knew it was my fault too.

I should have gotten Natalia's number and contact information before we hopped into bed together. But at that time, Natalia had been just another woman that was in and out of my life in a flash.

And my seed had germinated and blossomed into something precious beyond comprehension.

I was Bella's father.

And then there was Natalia. She had been working her magic on me from the first meeting. And I wondered how much of this pain could have been avoided if I had taken the time to think of why she had seemed so familiar. But when I first started with Prism Media, she had come off as just another workaholic prude. A gorgeous woman, but still not my type.

Then she had blossomed. But this time, it was in front of me. I admired her finesse in doing business. Her confidence and capabilities impressed me each time we crossed paths. Watching her work and how she could handle pretty much every situation had made me want her even more.

And then I'd gotten to have her not once, not twice, but more, and I could never get enough. She was like an addiction I couldn't break. She was on my mind more than any other woman ever had been. And she had just broken my heart.

How did I let myself become so open to feeling pain?

It was so against my nature and how I had been raised. *How did I let a woman of all things into my heart so she could ravage it at her will?*

I had begun to trust Natalia truly. I had decided that I would care for both her and Bella. Even when I thought Bella was the child of another man. But she was my child. I would never let her go now.

But what about Natalia? Do I want her intimately still? Could I ever trust her again?

I never let anyone who ruined my trust remain in my life. Tina and Terry could attest to that.

And I knew I could still be a father to Bella and cut Natalia out of my life. I could go for sole custody or even joint custody. I was not an unreasonable man. At least, I thought I wasn't. I didn't want to take Bella away from a mother who loved her, even if that woman had hurt me.

But I couldn't make up my mind about her, and it was driving me mad.

I wished I could talk to Terry. He would know the best thing to do and what my options were.

I wanted to take a week off work, but with Natalia out of the office as well, the whole building would probably be torn to bits. I wondered if I should put Vera in charge of operations. She was basically running everything herself already. But she would have a title to back her up and much higher pay. I made the decision and gave her a call.

"Vera speaking, Mr. Baxter. How are you?"

"Unwell," I said. "I need to take some time off. Is that feasible?"

She made a noise in her throat. "I am barely holding up as it is, and that is with Robert's help. I'd need more people and a person who can back up what I say for the bigger clients. They're a tough lot to deal with—all feel entitled to treat us like we are at their beck and call. Most of the staff are on two or three projects. They're not all ready to handle that much responsibility. I would recommend you hire at least three more people in Jason's assistant role and find me a board member to sign off on everything."

"You're the new board member. I'm hiring you as director of operations. Jason is now a manager of operations. Choose three staff members to work under him, and hire a few more project managers. Get the people you need. I am taking a week off."

"What about Miss Blake? Shouldn't she be here to help in your absence?" Vera asked.

"Miss Blake needs her time off. She has a family issue she needs to attend to. You can call her, though. Maybe she will come in."

"Can't you just call her for us?" Vera asked innocently.

Through gritted teeth, I said, "I'd rather not."

Vera clucked like a chicken and said, "I'll give her a call. The company needs at least one of you present, preferably both. Whatever is going on between you needs to be figured out. Thousands of jobs and the company depends on it."

I sputtered. "Excuse me?"

"The whole company knows there is something between you

two, down to the greenest intern. I suggest you two pull it together for the sake of the business."

I felt mortified and embarrassed that Vera had to reprimand me on my business acumen. And that all of the staff knew about Natalia's and my torrid little affair.

I briefly wondered what they would all think if it was revealed we had a four-year-old daughter together. We'd be the talk of the office for weeks.

"Sir?" Vera asked impatiently.

"Contact Miss Blake. I'm done for the week." I hung up the phone, sure that Natalia would go in. I knew she wouldn't want her empire to crumble.

I sat on my lounger in my home office. I could feel a headache coming on. I used to have them all the time when I was growing up. It had been years since I'd had one, but I clearly remembered what their onset felt like.

"Lee?" I called out. There was a slight rap at the door. I knew Lee wouldn't be far away. The man took his job almost too seriously.

"Yes, sir?"

"Would you grab me a big glass of water and a pain reliever?"

"Certainly." And he ghosted back out of the room. He came back sooner than expected. But I took two pills and chugged the water.

Before he left, I couldn't help but ask, "Lee? How was she after I left?"

Lee said, "To be honest, sir, it isn't my place to say."

"I suppose," I said, disappointed.

"She was dignified but had been crying. I will say no more." And with a quick bow, he made to exit the room.

"Thank you," I called after him.

I should have known not to ask my security detail about personal matters, but I couldn't help it. My inner turmoil was pulling me every which way.

One moment I was ragingly upset with Natalia and myself. The next, all I wanted to do was run there and claim her and Bella.

But did I want to claim a woman who didn't trust me enough to help raise my daughter? I picked up my phone and stared at it for a while. Then I dialed a number so familiar that I could have dialed it in my sleep.

"Cassius?" came the familiar baritone voice of my once best friend.

"Yes, Terry, it's me. Do you have a moment?"

"Of course. I'll always make time for you. What's up?"

I then began pouring my heart out to him. I started with Natalia's and my first encounter years ago. Terry knew I'd jumped from woman to woman for years. I told him over time, I had forgotten her. But she had never forgotten me.

And I told him about meeting her again at Prism Media and how she had never reminded me that we'd slept together. I told him how I couldn't blame her for doing what she did because I hadn't had any idea who she was to me.

I went into detail about our trip, scoring the biggest magazine merger in history and then making love to her in her gorgeous bright-blue bikini.

From there, I recalled us sharing intimate details about our lives. But when I looked back on it, I saw that Natalia had started closing up while I'd whined about how shitty my life was and how I'd said that, I hoped I never had a family, especially kids.

Terry was still listening at this point. He was letting me get it all out before interjecting with questions. The guy would have made an excellent counselor.

Then I spoke of how she suddenly took a month off with no explanation or warning and how I showed up at her house to find a small dark-haired child with ice-blue eyes and a crooked grin.

I heard Terry gasp at this. I could tell he'd caught the significance right away.

"I guess the time she took off work was because her child had stopped talking. But when I met the child, she had wanted to be picked up, and we talked about all the things that fascinate children. Then Natalia came out, and we all spent time together before putting her daughter to bed."

I described to Terry how upset I was that she had hid her child from me and how it had damaged some of the trust I was growing with her. Then I told him how we went out for dinner and how we'd talked about me remembering her. And then she'd dropped the bomb.

The thought rang through my head like a bell, worsening my headache. "She told me that Bella was my child. I was stunned but delighted. But then I realized what that meant for the relationship between Natalia and me."

"What does it mean?" Terry asked.

"That she didn't trust me. And that she didn't have enough faith in me to believe I would step up and be a proper father to Bella. And it got even worse when I realized she thought the bond and relationship we were building was not as genuine as I'd believed it was."

"Why do you say that?"

"Because she never told me, all this time. She wasn't sure if I was being honest with her and then omitted the fact we had a child together. It was my right to know, no matter what was happening between us. A father deserves to know his child, even if the child's parents hate each other."

Then I told him the magazine project was falling apart since we had both taken time off right in the middle of the merger. I felt like a complete ass. I had always put business first and personal life later. Now was not the time to sit around and mope. "So, what do you think?" I asked Terry, hungry for his advice.

"I think you have a shot of getting something pure and true into your life, and you are letting your brain and ego get in the way of everything. You have a daughter, and yes, you missed a chunk of her childhood, but there are a good fifteen years of raising her before she's an adult. Plenty of time to be a good influence in her life. And she is young enough that she will be happy to have a daddy."

"And what about Natalia? Should I forgive her?"

Terry sighed deeply. "This is where I cannot provide you with an unbiased viewpoint. As one who has hurt you in the past, I want you to forgive her because maybe that would mean I will have a shot at being forgiven too. I miss you, buddy."

I got choked up for a second and couldn't think of anything to say.

"Follow what's in your heart, Cassius. If you can imagine a life sharing a child with her but in two separate households and each having periods where Bella will be with the other parent, then go that route. But if the thought of sharing Bella as a family all living together appeals to you, then I believe you should continue your relationship with Natalia. Give it patience and time, but eventually, things should work out."

"Thank you, Terry. You've been helpful, as always."

"Another thing, I agree with what she did—waiting to see how things with you would turn out. She was afraid of losing her daughter. That does something to people. When it comes to their kids, parents don't always act rationally. I think you should forgive her and be happy she was protecting your child, even if it was from you."

I was silent after that declaration. Terry had a way of looking at things from the other person's point of view. God, I missed having him in my life. Up until he'd slept with Tina, he had been my number one confidant.

I felt a tear slide down my cheek. I quickly wiped it away, unsure whether it was for the loss of Terry or what he'd said. Maybe it was a bit of both. His advice was always the best.

"Thank you for the advice, Terry. I am sorry we had a falling out. But you know me. Forgiveness is hard for me to swallow sometimes."

"Cassius, I don't expect you to forgive me immediately. After the trust is broken, it is reasonable to feel hurt and distrustful. But I hope that someday, you will fully forgive me. Until then, it's something we can work toward. I suggest we try and catch up once in a while and see what happens. I want to be friends again. I've missed your companionship."

"Thank you for talking to me. I needed someone, and you were there for me like you used to be."

Terry let loose a whoosh of air. "I will always be here for you. I promise."

We hung up the phone. I still didn't know what to do. But I felt better after getting it off my chest. And what Terry had said resonated with me. *Would I have done the same if I were in Natalia's shoes?* Yes, I really might have.

I was still sitting in my lounger. I realized my headache had gone away, and I was regaining my second wind. I supposed I should work out, and I stood up and walked to the gym.

My mind was full of Bella and Natalia. That one afternoon with them had delighted me. I wanted that all the time.

I missed Natalia—how she threw her head back when she laughed, how she looked at her hands when she was nervous. I loved her beautiful smile and even how gorgeous she still looked when crying. But I loved her warm heart and generous nature to all. I missed her, and it hadn't even been a full day.

And then there was Bella. I wanted to hug her right that second, pick her up and play with her, show her the life I had always wanted.

As I started doing my crunches, I realized how empty my life was. Without Terry, I had no one. Worse, without Natalia and Bella, my life was incomplete. I felt a hollowness I had never noticed before and vowed that one way or another, I would be whole soon.

Chapter Twenty-Two

NATALIA

"**M**ama?" Bella asked. "Can I see Cas-sus again?"

Those were the last words I had expected to hear from Bella as I drove her to her day care. I swerved the car a bit in shock. "I'm not sure, honey. Hopefully, you will get to soon." I doubted it, but Cassius had surprised me more than once throughout the course of our relationship. I expected him to want to see his daughter at some point. I just wondered when that would be.

When I'd received Vera's panicky call, I had been disappointed to hear that Cassius had taken an impromptu vacation when the business needed him. And despite all my reservations, I decided the best thing to do was step back up to the plate and get down to doing my job.

Bella was okay now. She was a resilient child. As I drove to her day care, I said, "And what do you do if the boy makes fun of you?"

"I find a teacher and tell them."

"Good, baby girl."

"Mama, I am not a baby anymore," Bella said seriously.

I looked at her through the rearview mirror. The determined

expression on her face reminded me of Cassius. I couldn't help but smile. "I know, Bella. You're a big girl now." I watched as she nodded in satisfaction.

I pulled into the day care's parking lot, got out of the car, and helped Bella out of her booster seat. She hugged and kissed me, then grabbed her little pink book bag and walked to the door holding my hand. We were greeted at the door by Miss Vickie, the day care owner.

"Welcome back, Bella. I am happy to see you."

Bella was acting a bit shy, not meeting the woman's eyes, but she politely said, "Thank you, Miss Vickie. I am happy to see you too."

The older woman winked at me, then took Bella by the hand. "Say goodbye to your mother."

Bella waved and began walking inside. I climbed into the SUV, waiting to ensure they got into the building. And once they did, I headed to the office. Rory was going to pick her up after day care while I sorted out the mess at work.

I expected it to be a long day.

When I pulled into my designated parking spot at the office, I couldn't help but notice that Cassius's parking spot was empty. Part of me wanted to call him up right then and there. But I wanted to respect his wishes and give him the time he needed to reconcile our differences and for him to step up and assume the role of a father. I couldn't blame him for wanting some time to himself.

I expected everyone in the office to be running around like chickens with their heads cut off but was pleasantly surprised to see everyone diligently working away. I headed to my office and noticed that two of the larger offices were now occupied. One was filled with stacks of files, and Vera was seated at the large desk scribbling on some papers.

"Hi, Vera. I see you've climbed the corporate chain fast."

"No offense, Miss Blake, but someone had to step up and start running the place. We need you and Mr. Baxter, and I will be honest and say that we have really struggled without proper leadership."

I felt properly chastened. "I appreciate all your hard work. And congratulations on your new role. Who is in the other office?"

"Robert Hilson. He became my assistant and is now a manager. The young man has a strong work ethic." Vera was collecting a large stack of file folders. She then passed the pile to me. "These are all the files that need your approval and signature. Trinda has more for you in your office. Will you be staying at work for the next week or so? That's how long Mr. Baxter said his time off would be."

I grabbed the hefty stack of files and said, "I will do what I must." Once again, I thanked her before heading to my office.

As I approached, Trinda looked up, greeted me briefly, then focused again on whatever she was working on. I opened the door to my office and saw a whole cart full of files. I sighed heavily, then got down to work.

By the time lunch came, I had put a dent in the files, but Trinda had brought in more. I couldn't help but sigh and rub my head. I was getting a headache. I took some painkillers and ordered lunch from my favorite sushi place.

Soon it was three o'clock. I expected to hear from Rory soon. I had wanted to be the one to pick Bella up, but as it was, I didn't have enough hours in the day to finish my workload. I would be bringing home boxes of files in order to catch up.

My phone rang. I checked the caller ID and saw that it was Rory. "Hey, Rory, how was Bella's first day back?"

"What? I am at the day care now. They said they think you picked her up a half hour ago."

"No, I didn't. I'm still at work."

"I'll call you right back," he said, hanging up on me.

I sat staring at the phone in my hand. There had to be some

sort of mistake. I set the cell down and began going over another brief. The phone rang again.

"Bella is gone!" Rory said, panic laced through his voice.

"That's not funny, Rory. Bella has to be there somewhere. Maybe she is hiding." I kept my voice calm, though my chest clenched. I could feel my anxiety seeping into my gut.

"We have searched the entire day care and the park the kids went to today. She is nowhere to be found." Rory's voice was shaky.

This wasn't a joke. I stood up, briefs falling to the floor. I robotically grabbed my purse and car keys. "I'm on my way," I said into the phone, then hung up. I left my office, not even bothering to lock it.

"Trinda," I said as I passed her desk. "There's a family emergency I have to take care of. I'll be back as soon as I can."

"Is there anything I can do to help?" she asked. "Miss Blake, you're shaking. Are you okay? Do you need a ride somewhere?"

I looked at my hand where my keys jangled. She was right. I was shaking. "Can you take me to my daughter's day care? I don't trust myself to drive right now." I felt a hollowness inside. Like I was insubstantial. I kept telling myself it was all a big misunderstanding and that they will have found Bella by the time I arrived at the day care.

Trinda grabbed her things, and we exited the building quickly.

"What happened?" she asked once we were outside of the building.

"They can't find my daughter." I watched Trinda's gray eyes widen.

She asked the address and sped the whole way there. When we arrived, a police cruiser was pulling up, and a pair of cops were talking to Miss Vickie, whose eyes were red with tears. Rory was standing there as well, arms crossed against his chest.

He looked up as I got out of Trinda's car. He had a guilty

expression on his face and looked toward the ground as if ashamed. I walked measuredly to the police.

"Have you found her?" I asked.

Rory shook his head.

"Are you the mother?" one of the officers asked.

I nodded, afraid to speak, worried that I would burst into tears and have a nervous breakdown on the spot.

"We have no specific timeline for when she disappeared. She was with them when they left the park because they did a head count. But from then on, they can't be sure."

I nodded again, swallowing hard. "How long ago was that?" I squeaked out the question.

"Two to three hours," Miss Vickie spoke up. "I am so sorry, Miss Blake. She was doing really well today. She was playful and chatty. I kept an eye on her, but then she was just gone. We've searched everywhere, and there is no sign of her. All her stuff is still here." She proffered Bella's backpack, and I took it from her lily-white hands.

I rummaged through it. "Bella's pink teddy bear isn't here. Did you find it?" I looked up at everyone who encircled me.

"No," Miss Vickie said. "It wasn't inside."

"She never goes anywhere without it." My voice broke on the last word, then the dam of tears broke, and I realized I had fallen to my knees.

Rory was there, hugging me. His face was also wet. "We will find her," Rory reassured me.

"We need pictures, and we will put out an Amber Alert," the officer said.

Miss Vickie ran inside and came back out with a picture of Bella. One officer took the image and went to the car.

Rory helped me back to my feet. My knees wobbled. I had to keep my cool, so I wiped my eyes and forced myself to stand upright.

"Ma'am?" the police officer said, addressing me. "Is there

anyone who would take the child? Maybe a family member or a friend?"

"We have no other family members in town," I said, wiping my eyes with the backs of my hand. Mascara smudges were all over them.

"What about the father?" the officer asked. "Is he in the picture?"

My mouth dropped open, and I instantly began digging in my purse. I pulled out my phone and dialed Cassius. He answered after a few rings.

"Natalia," he said in a serious tone, "I thought I asked you for some time."

"Please tell me you took Bella."

"Bella? Why would I take Bella? What happened?"

"She's missing, Cassius."

"Where are you? I'll be right there." He hung up after I gave him the address.

I turned to the police officer, and my lip trembled. "Her father is on his way."

All the phones in the vicinity started going off. The Amber Alert must have been sent out. I looked at my phone to see a lovely image of Bella hugging her favorite teddy bear. I burst into tears again, but I did not fall this time. I had to find her.

And then another thought hit me. It was the woman in the wig. She had threatened to hurt Bella and me if I didn't stay away from Cassius. *Was this her doing?*

I picked up the phone and redialed Cassius. "The woman in a wig who threatened me, would she do this?"

He stayed silent for a long moment. "I'll call you right back." And then he hung up the phone.

I began telling the police about the woman, how she'd had me followed and had threatened me by showing me pictures of me and Bella. I couldn't give an accurate description or even her name, but they took the information down, including the police report I had already filed.

Another police cruiser showed up, this time with a K-9 unit.

"We are going to search the perimeter. Please have a seat and wait patiently. We are doing all we can to find your daughter."

I didn't feel reassured, but I sat on the steps of the day care.

A few minutes later, my phone rang again. It was Cassius.

"I tried to get in touch with her, but her phone went right to voicemail. I have had a security detail tailing you, and two of the men have not reported in for well over an hour."

There was suddenly a commotion. The dogs were barking. I dropped the phone and ran toward the noise. When I got there, I saw a body lying on the ground. I ran to it, terrified it was Bella. But as I approached, a police officer grabbed me.

"It's not your daughter," the female officer said, holding me tightly. "We did find the bear, though. We are taking it in as evidence. This is now a homicide case."

I heard car tires squeal. Cassius had arrived.

I tore out of the policewoman's grip and ran toward the sound of Cassius's car engine turning off. When he was right in front of me, I froze. I didn't know how to act. Part of me wanted to run into his arms, and the other part reminded me that he was still mad at my actions and choices.

The funny thing was, he froze too. We stared at each other across the expanse. And then I watched his face crumple, his armor failing. He rushed over to me and picked me up as he hugged me.

He whispered into my hair, "I'm so sorry, Natalia." Then he kissed me with lips that tasted salty from his tears.

I then noticed the small Asian man standing behind Cassius. "Sir?" he asked, "May I go check on my team?" Cassius gave a wordless nod, and the slight man headed toward the alley in the back of the house.

"Cassius," I said breathily, "whoever took Bella killed a security

guard to get at her. They found her teddy bear near the body."
Fresh tears spilled out of my eyes.

"I promise you," he said, gripping my chin in his hand. "We will find her."

"How?"

"I think I know who took her," he replied with chagrin. "It's my ex, Tina."

"The one who threatened me?" I was astounded. "I didn't take her seriously. And I figured once she had her say, she would back off. Do you think she would actually kill a man to get to Bella and me?"

The look on his face said it all.

The Asian man came back around the corner, his expression grave. "It was one of my men," he said. "One man is still missing. Whoever did this had help."

I knew I had a confused look on my face.

Cassius spoke up. "A friend warned me that Tina was losing her mind and had threatened you, so I put a security detail in charge of supervising you two. Two stayed with Bella, and two with you. I'm sorry. I should have told you earlier."

I could only stand there in shock. It was too unreal to think that someone hated me enough to steal the most important thing in my life.

"We should start searching for her. I know a few places where she could be holed up. The whole city knows she is missing, thanks to the Amber Alert. Someone would have seen them. Come with me while we search. The police can handle the crime scene here."

Robotically, I got into the passenger side of the car. The Asian man, who introduced himself formally as Lee, slipped into the small back seat.

Rory came up to the window, and I rolled it down.

"I'll stay here then head back home just in case someone drops her off or finds her here," he intoned. Rory, as always, remained calm and said to me, "Someone will find her. I know she is okay."

Then he gave me an awkward hug through the window, and Cassius, Lee, and I began our long search for my—no our—child. I then noticed a black SUV behind us.

"Who is that?" I pointed out the vehicle.

"That's my security detail and yours. We expect that both of Bella's guards were taken out. Though, one is still missing."

I felt myself getting angry at the guards who had failed, even though I knew it wasn't their fault. One man had lost his life for the sake of my child. Bella's loss started to hit me at that point, and I began having a panic attack and hyperventilating.

"Take it easy," Cassius said, reaching out to hold my hand. "We will find her. Our first stop will be a few of the art stores and warehouses she owns. It is most likely that she would hole up in one of those places."

But after driving for hours and having the security team raid those buildings, we still ended up empty-handed.

As the light of day began dimming, I still wanted to be searching, but we needed to eat and recover. With each stop we made, my hopes would lift, and watching the security team return without her brought my grief back into the foremost part of my mind.

Where is my baby girl?

Against my better judgment, we went through a drive-through to grab ourselves a meal. I bought a kid's meal just in case we found Bella. Cassius eyed me as he passed it to me but didn't comment. I knew it was wishful thinking. Tina could have holed up anywhere, but I needed to cling to the hope we would find her.

"Cassius," I said, "what happened between you and Tina that she would kill someone and steal my child."

"I broke up with her for sleeping with my best friend," he said, eyes not leaving the road. "I think she expected me to take her back, but I cut all ties and even changed my number. I guess she finally realized I was serious."

"So this is your fault."

He spun on me, almost driving the car off the road. "This is not my fault, Natalia. I didn't steal Bella. A psycho did."

That didn't do much to make me feel better. But Cassius was right. I couldn't blame him. But when I saw this woman, I wanted to claw her eyes out.

We checked five more buildings, and soon it was almost midnight. I leaned back in my seat and realized I had fallen asleep when we went over a bump.

"It's time to call it a night and get some rest so we can start early tomorrow," Cassius said.

I noticed his cheeks were glistening. I knew he felt responsible, despite what he had said.

I reached out a hand and rested it on his lap. "I think you're right," I said to Cassius. "I want to go home. I know if she had been found, Rory would have called, but I want to sleep in her bed."

"May I join you?" he asked tentatively.

I could only nod, not trusting myself to speak. "I have one spare room for Lee to sleep in if he wants."

"That will not be necessary, miss. I am on the job." I liked the sound of his accent, and there was something soothing to it. "I will be guarding the premises with my teammates. The shift changes soon, and the other guard still hasn't been found. When we find him, we may figure out where the woman took your child."

Cassius was soon pulling up to my home. I saw that the lights were still on, and Rory was up. The SUV pulled into the driveway, and the men dispersed to various corners of the property. Cassius came around the car and opened the door for me. He held out his hand, and I put mine in his. He gently lifted me out of the vehicle into his arms.

"You don't have to do this, Cassius," I said.

"I can tell how tired you are. Let me bring you inside."

I didn't bother resisting. I leaned my head on his chest and sighed. It felt nice to be carried. Rory opened the door for us and greeted us quickly before heading in the direction of his room.

Cassius brought me directly to Bella's room and laid me down. It was a double bed, so he lay down beside me and began rubbing my head. I curled up against his chest, and the tears started again. He lifted my chin, and his lips pressed firmly against mine.

"We will find her, Natalia. Now rest."

I relaxed and drifted off into the peace of sleep.

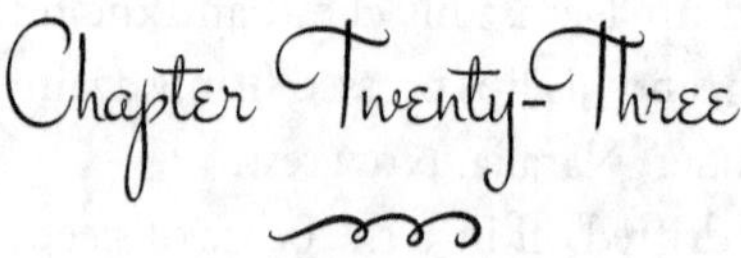

CASSIUS

I woke early and found Natalia curled up in my arms. I felt like I hadn't moved all night. My body was achy, as was my heart. I couldn't begin to explain how horrible I felt. If I had only done something different, this whole situation could have been avoided.

I gazed at Natalia as she breathed deeply. Her long black eyelashes fluttered as if she were dreaming. I kissed her forehead and breathed in her scent. It was almost citrusy. She suddenly jerked and opened her milk-chocolate eyes. They were bloodshot and puffy, but the desperation in them made my gut clench.

"No news?" she asked.

I shook my head. "They would have woken us."

Her face darkened. "We have to get out there again. She has to be somewhere you know. Is there anywhere else we haven't checked?"

"Not many more places. I think it's time I bring in someone who has been close to Tina over the past year. Even though I still don't want to involve him, I think it's our best bet."

"Who?" she queried.

"Terry. The best friend she cheated on me with."

"Oh." She sat up and brushed her hair out of her face. "Let's get ready and go."

"Do you want to shower or anything? Eat?" I asked, noticing how worn she looked. "It might make you feel better."

"Nothing will make me feel better while that psycho has my child, Cassius." The look she gave me was angry, but she turned away, crawled out of the small bed, and left the bedroom.

I followed her, and she turned into her bedroom.

"I'm going to change my clothes. Meet me in the kitchen. See if Rory can make us a few sandwiches to go. I want to continue the search. And you need to get in contact with Terry. If there is even a chance that he knows, we have to take it."

I nodded and walked downstairs.

Rory was already in the kitchen. His brown hair was tousled, and his nut-brown eyes were piercing when he glanced at me. "Morning," he mumbled. "I am making some food for you guys for while you're out searching. And the police called, saying they have posters of Bella to disperse. I'll do that today. I can't bear to sit here waiting any longer."

"I don't blame you. Thank you for thinking ahead. I have to make a phone call." I exited the kitchen and went outside.

I dialed Terry's number. "Terry?" I asked immediately.

"Cassius?"

"Yes, it's me. Have you seen an Amber Alert on your phone?"

"Yes."

"That's my child, Terry. We believe Tina stole her and possibly harmed her. One man is already dead. This is serious. I need your help. Where would Tina take a child if she didn't want to be found?"

Terry was silent for a long moment. "Did you try all the warehouses she owns?"

"Yes, well, at least all the ones I know about. All were empty. Is there anywhere else?"

"Where are you?" he asked.

"At Natalia's place. We're leaving shortly, but I have no idea where to start looking."

"What's the address? I will be right over. We can go together."

I was hesitant initially but then decided I had no other option. Terry knew Tina and the way her mind worked. He was also the only person I knew she had spoken with recently. I gave him the address and went back inside.

Natalia was dressed in jeans and a blue tank top when I reentered the kitchen. She looked beautiful, despite the unkemptness of her hair and the fact that she wasn't wearing any makeup.

"Did you contact him?" she asked immediately, hope in her eyes.

"Yes, he's on his way to help. He has a few ideas, I think, and he knows Tina. He may be able to talk some sense into her. At least, that's what I am hoping." I shrugged. "I have no idea where to look next."

She began helping Rory again. They were packing a lot of food and some of Bella's things, like her blanket and a stuffed rabbit, in case she was found.

"We're taking my vehicle. It seats more people and has Bella's car seat." Natalia grabbed a bag off the counter and made her way out to her SUV.

She loaded the trunk, and Rory brought out a cooler. He let us know that there were drinks, sandwiches, and a few heartier meals in plastic containers. He brought a smaller second cooler to his old blue truck, gripping a file folder filled with missing posters.

"I'll be distributing these all day. If anything happens, call me and let me know." With that, he got into the truck and took off.

Lee wasn't on duty, but the security staff they had assigned for today seemed to hold themselves more alert. There were two SUVs full, and they were ready for some serious ops. Their equipment was more advanced, as was their protective gear. The guns they carried had some strong firepower.

I saw Terry's car coming down the road. One of the security guards halted him in the middle of the street.

"It's okay," I called. "He's with us!"

They let him through, eyeing the big, bald man warily. Terry looked intimidating to anyone who didn't know him. He was tall and muscular with brooding eyes. He drove his blue jeep into the driveway and hopped out, heading straight for me.

"I have a few ideas," he said immediately. I liked how Terry always cut to the chase. "She has been attending raves a lot lately. She's hooked on something, but I don't know what. Whatever it is, I think it's what made her lose her mind. These raves are in a variety of spots. I'll take you to the few I know of." He turned around and stepped up into his jeep.

I hadn't noticed, but Natalia had come up behind me.

"Did you hear him?" I asked her.

She nodded, then went to her SUV. "Today, I'm driving. Get in." She basically barked at me. I got in without a word and did up my seatbelt.

"Just follow him," I said.

Terry's jeep pulled away, and Natalia reversed out of the driveway like a pro. She was right on top of him the entire ride.

We pulled into a warehouse that was in a bad part of the city. There was graffiti everywhere, and the building was made of old gray stone. Terry came up to us as we got out of the vehicle as the security team was talking about strategies. Two people were being sent ahead to scout.

As they had done the other twenty times we searched buildings for Bella, they told us to stay back and wait for a signal. It was torturous. I wanted to help, but I had hired them for a reason, so I let them do their jobs.

Once again, the scouts came out saying they hadn't found anyone. The rest of the team dispersed throughout the building, checking every nook and cranny. But as always, Bella and Tina were nowhere to be found. Natalia turned her head away. I saw her chest rise and fall as she choked back sobs.

"It will be okay, my sweet." I wrapped myself around her and rubbed her back with my hand. "We will find Bella, and she will be okay. We've still got a couple more spots to check. She will be at one of them. I can feel it."

She didn't say anything but moved my arms away so she could climb back into the SUV. She looked like she was losing hope. We all knew that the longer Bella was gone, the more unlikely she was to be found. But I kept reminding myself that Terry would know where she was.

We followed him to the next location. It was another warehouse but in a slightly better area. A car was parked in the driveway. Terry pointed to it and laid a finger against his lips. It was Tina's.

The security team surrounded us. In hushed voices, they said, "We will proceed as usual. But we know that they may be in this building. We will give you the signal when you should approach."

"Let's go with them, Cassius." Natalia's eyes were pleading. "Bella won't know these men. She will be as scared of them as she will be of Tina."

"Natalia, I want to go in there as much as you, but we can't. Let the professionals handle it."

"Fuck that," said a deep voice from behind us. "Tina may shoot if she thinks she's being taken in by the police or a special ops team. Together, we may have a chance of taking her down and keeping the kid safe." Terry pulled out a silver-colored gun that I recognized as his prized Desert Eagle.

Then he handed me his Glock. "I am not taking that thing in there," I said, gesturing for him to keep it.

He then passed it to Natalia. I expected her to hand it back, but she quickly checked the chamber and the magazine.

I looked at her like I had no idea who she was. "Where did you learn to do that?" I asked, shock filling my voice.

"My father," she answered simply. "He used to take me hunting, and he's a gun collector. As his only child, he taught me."

Terry gave me a grin. "I like this one," he said, thumbing in Natalia's direction.

"I won't have you three endangering my men," said the head honcho of the security team. "Wait one minute, then follow us. We will secure the rooms and lead the way. When we find them, then you can try to talk her down. But you better stay behind us. Got it?"

The three of us nodded, and the team scattered to different points of the building. There were five stories, and the yard was littered with bottles, clothing, and junk. We made our way to an entry point and began silently stalking behind the security team. I was impressed at how swiftly they worked. They cleared room after room, giving each other hand signals as they went. I was happy to see I'd spent my money wisely.

We were on our way to the third floor when we heard a screech. Everyone paused. The sound was almost inhuman.

Stay here, one of the guards mouthed to us.

They went up the stairs on silent feet and out of view. We waited for a few minutes, then one of them popped their head around the corner and waved us forward. We rushed up the stairs.

When we were close, one said quietly, "They are on the fourth floor, and all we see are the woman and child. Two of the guards are checking the top floor, but we believe they are alone."

I glanced at Natalia; her eyes glistened in the faint light.

She gave me a nervous grin. "We can save her," she whispered fiercely.

"Don't do anything crazy. In fact," I whispered, "stay behind us. If Tina sees you, she might do something drastic. Stay out of sight for Bella's sake."

The severe look on her face made me shiver. "If anyone shoots Tina, I want it to be me," she said determinedly.

"You're going to jeopardize your daughter if Tina sees you,"

Terry said, laying a hand on her shoulder. "She is not in her right mind. That means Tina is unpredictable. She may see you and shoot Bella, and I know you do not want that."

Natalia glanced at me, then back at Terry before nodding in agreement. I mentally thanked Terry. I would owe him big time for all the help he had provided.

"Please, just stay here," I said to her. "We will be back soon. Just stay safe, for Bella's sake."

"I'm coming up to the fourth floor with you, but I will stay at the top of the stairs." I gave her a doubtful look, and she snapped, "I promise."

"Follow us," the guard said, and Terry and I followed in silence.

The hallway was littered with refuse, and the air smelled of cigarettes and liquor. There must have been a rave here recently, judging by the state of the place. I glanced into a room and saw a prone figure lying there. I grabbed Terry's shoulder and pointed into the room. His eyes opened wide, and he tapped the guard on the shoulder, pointing into the room.

"Dead by gunshot," the guard whispered. "And recently," he added.

I went into the room and rolled the corpse over. It was the man who had been following me. He had been shot in the chest at point-blank range. Tina must have realized he was a liability or that she didn't need him anymore. Whatever the reason, Tina was now a murderer. And if she'd killed once, she would do it again.

The fear I felt for my daughter had me shaking. I wanted the gun now. I was tempted to go back and get it, but the security guard was waving at us to come close.

As we approached, he whispered, "The two of them are in a big room at the center of the building. It has two entryways. One of you should enter one way, and the other should head to the other entrance. Since she knows you two, we think she may not shoot. Right now, the kid is sitting in the center of the room.

The woman is circling her with a gun in hand. Try to talk her down."

"I'll talk to her," I said. "Terry, you go through the other entrance while I keep her distracted. Try to grab her from behind."

He nodded, and the security guard pointed Terry in the other direction. We gave each other a parting nod, and I went to face the woman who had stolen my child.

Every step seemed to take hours, and I knew this situation could go horribly wrong with any of us getting shot or killed. The security guard pointed at a lit doorway. I felt tense and inadequately prepared for this showdown.

I peeked around the corner and saw that the security guard had given an accurate description. Bella was seated on the granite floor with her arms wrapped around herself. One of her tear-stained cheeks was swollen and bruised. The bitch had hit my child. I instantly felt enraged, ready to run into the room and choke Tina to death.

Tina had on a bathrobe of all things. Underneath, she wore what looked like a corset. Her hair was short and wild. I had rarely seen her without her wig, but judging by the mousey-brown color, I could see why she wore one. Compared to the last time I'd seen her, her face was gaunt, as if she hadn't eaten properly for weeks. She was circling Bella in slow, measured steps.

It was now or never. I stood straight and walked into the entrance, calling, "Tina?"

She turned, and the gun went off, hitting the wall beside me. I covered my ringing ears. The sound was so loud and close to me that it hurt.

"Tina, it's me, Cassius."

She was pointing the gun at me, and she was shaking violently. "Is that bitch here with you?" she screamed at me.

"No," I said, "It's just me. Let the girl go, please. Do it for me."

"No. Did you know she was your child this whole time? Why didn't you tell me about her?" she wailed.

"That's not my child, Tina. It's my coworker's kid." I would have told her the sky was pink just to get Bella back safely.

"Liar!" she screamed and shot again at me. This time, I felt the bullet graze my arm. Blood welled up, soaking my shirt.

"Stop, Tina!" I yelled.

But she wasn't listening. She hauled Bella up by the hair and pointed the gun at my child's head. I could feel my adrenaline rushing, and I wanted to lunge for the two of them, but then I caught sight of Terry creeping up behind them slowly.

I had to keep her distracted. "Please, Tina. I want you back. Just let the child go, and we can be together."

"No," she said. "I've done bad things. There is no going back now. I need to end it. End it all."

"Tina," I begged, "please, just come to me. We can leave this city and be together. We can go anywhere you want."

She looked at me, considering. Then I watched the gun drop down from Bella's head. Terry was almost there. A few more steps, and he would have her.

"Please, Tina. Come with me," I said coaxingly, giving her a come-here gesture. "We can be on a plane headed out of the country in an hour."

I watched as she released Bella's hair, and I don't know what made her do it, but she looked over her shoulder. Her face contorted as she attempted to twirl around and raise the gun. But Terry wrapped his big arms around her, pinning her arms to her sides.

I ran and scooped Bella into my arms, sheltering her with my body.

The gun dropped from Tina's hand and went off when it hit the ground. I heard Terry grunt in pain. The security team poured into the room, securing the weapon and pushing Tina down face-first onto the floor. One guard held her down with a knee and bound her arms behind her with a plastic tie. She squirmed and screamed.

Terry was gripping his thigh where the bullet had entered. He was losing blood fast. I wanted to go to him, but I still held Bella to my chest, who was sobbing and crying for her mother.

"Bella!" I heard Natalia cry from behind me. She ran to us and wrapped her arms around Bella.

I released my hold and said, "I have to see to Terry. Go to the car and stay there."

She nodded and picked up Bella and left the room.

I turned to Terry, where a security guard was placing pressure on the wound. I unbuckled my belt and wrapped it above the bullet's entry point. "It'll be okay, Terry. The police will be on their way."

"I already called them when we first caught sight of Tina and the girl," a guard said.

Then I realized I could hear the sirens.

"See, Terry? Everything will be okay." I was worried about the pale color of his face and the rapidly expanding pool of blood.

"We are square now, buddy," I reassured him.

"Honestly?" he asked.

Tina's screams cut out as a guard taped her mouth shut.

"I give you my word. If Tina had been the one, she wouldn't have done that to us. And if you hadn't done that, I would still be trapped in a relationship with that nut job." I looked at Tina, whose eyes were drilling holes into me. "We are both better off."

Terry nodded and looked toward Tina. "I am still sorry."

"Don't be," I said. "You've made me the happiest man in the world. I have a family now. I feel like a hole has been filled."

Terry grinned, and then I turned toward the commotion as the police entered the room with the paramedics hard on their heels.

"That's nice to hear, Cass." Terry's head fell forward onto his chest, his eyes closing.

I pressed my ear to his chest, listening for his heart. Terror gripped me.

The paramedics kneeled beside us and began working on Terry.

"He still has a heart rate, and the blood loss is slowing. Let us get him to the hospital," a paramedic said, pushing me away.

I stood up, blood soaking my pants, just in time to see the cops removing the tape from Tina's mouth.

She started screaming at me, "You're a liar, Cassius Baxter. I'll see you dead!" The police escorted her out of the room. I could hear her screaming the whole way out of the building.

Soon, Terry was on a stretcher and wheeled out of the room. I followed but took the time to look out the window. Two ambulances were parked in the yard and multiple police vehicles. Two officers were speaking with Natalia while Bella sat in the back of an ambulance.

I had to get down there fast. I ran the entire way, and when I burst out of the doorway, Natalia rushed forward to meet me. She jumped into my arms and sobbed loudly. I just held her as she repeatedly thanked me.

She pulled back, and we watched as Terry's ambulance left the warehouse yard.

"Please tell me none of that is your blood," she said, running her hands around my body.

"No, it's Terry's. He saved Bella."

"Is he going to be okay?" she asked concernedly.

"I hope so."

"You can't see Bella while you're all covered in blood. They're taking her to the hospital too. I'll go in the ambulance. You take my SUV and get changed. Then meet us there." She rose on her tippy-toes and kissed me on the cheek. "Thank you, Cassius. You saved my daughter. I don't know how to thank you."

"Our daughter, Natalia."

"Yes, Cassius, our daughter."

Her delighted smile made me grin, and I pulled her close and kissed her as if I never had before.

NATALIA

I held Bella tightly the entire way to the hospital. I crawled right up on the stretcher, not wanting to be more than a few inches from her. I held her as she cried silently. Kissing the bruise on her cheek, I started repeating to her that she was safe. But I didn't think she believed me. Her chubby little fingers squeezed my shirt as if she was afraid to let go, and she buried her face into my chest.

I wished I could just take her home. Getting abducted was traumatic enough, but I wanted her thoroughly checked out for her safety, and we needed evidence to charge Tina with assault and kidnapping. That woman would get what was coming to her.

My compassion for the woman was gone the minute I saw she'd laid hands on my daughter. At first, I'd pitied her, but then I'd been filled with a rage I had never felt before. I could have strangled the woman with my bare hands. And my adrenaline was through the roof.

When we got to the hospital, the paramedics didn't even ask me to get off the stretcher. I think they knew how important it was for me to hold Bella.

Bella hadn't spoken a word to me. I was terrified that she

would pull into herself even deeper and never talk again. I wouldn't blame her. Being kidnapped and held at gunpoint would be traumatizing to an adult, let alone a little girl.

I prayed for Cassius to hurry up. I would feel better with him around, and I hoped he could help break Bella out of her shell faster. I would have to make an appointment with Mrs. VanAllen again soon. After this, I was sure that Bella would require years of therapy.

A doctor came to look at Bella right away. He said she would need tests for further injury caused by the blow to her face. And when he pulled up her pants to look at her legs, Bella started crying harder. The reason shocked me. Her legs were covered in bruises and scrapes as if she had been repeatedly thrown to the ground.

My hate for Tina flared. Hell wouldn't be enough of a punishment for her.

I helped slip Bella into a johnny shirt and helped the Doctor tend to the various scrapes. Her arms and torso were covered with a smattering of purples and reds. It took a while for each injury to be assessed, cleaned, and wrapped.

Then Cassius walked into the room. One look at Bella made his face darken, but when Bella looked up and saw who had arrived, she instantly raised her arms to be picked up.

Relief permeated my being. I had been worried that Bella would be afraid of Cassius, but his wet hair, clean khakis, and white sweater made him look soothing and inviting. Cassius calmly walked over and scooped Bella into his arms.

"Hi, Cass-us," Bella said softly before hugging him around the neck.

I couldn't help but make a sound in my throat. It thrilled me that she was speaking again. I had expected days of silence.

"I'll have a nurse take her to X-ray for a CT scan," the doctor said, "after you and your family take some time to be together."

"We'd rather get on with it so we can return home sooner," Cassius said.

The doctor nodded knowingly. "I'll send the porter right away."

They allowed Cassius and me to stay with Bella until she went into the X-ray room, and when she came out, she had a pink teddy bear clutched in her hands.

"Where did you get that?" I asked her.

She acted shyly for a moment, chewing on her finger while looking thoughtful. "The nurse gave it to me," she then said quietly.

"That's so nice of her. Did you thank her?"

"Yes, Mama."

"What are you going to name it?" asked Cassius, who tenderly pushed Bella's hair over her shoulder.

She looked like she was having difficulty deciding before she spit out, "Berry."

"That's a great name," I said, knowing that she was being clever. I wondered if she was showing off for Cassius or really wanted to name the bear that. I decided it was a bit of both.

The X-ray went fine, but she started screaming during the CT scan when they made her lie on the table. The doctor arrived quickly, and they sedated her. He also gave her a shot of pain reliever.

"I don't know if the trauma or the injuries bothered her, so I gave her something that helps with both," the doctor told us.

This time when she went through the CT scan, she was on the verge of falling asleep.

We were taken back to the room, and it was a wait for the results. When the doctor finally came back, he told us she had a concussion and a fracture in her forearm. He arranged for her to get a cast, and they wrapped it up while she was still asleep.

I was amazed at how tough she was, and I mentioned it to Cassius.

"That's because she's your daughter," he said with a chuckle.

"It's amazing how you don't even seem to see the resemblance between you two."

"I can't believe you didn't realize she was yours the second you met her," I said. "She's the spitting image of you."

Cassius looked at her and said, "All I saw in her was you." The look he gave me then was surprisingly gentle, and his eyes were brimming in tears. "I am so sorry I brought this on you two."

I didn't say a word in response. I looked down at my hands and realized how jagged my nails were. I had been chewing them without even realizing it. I couldn't bring myself to say it was fine. Anger over what Tina had done to my child made me want to lash out, but I knew Cassius had done much to protect us and then help me find Bella. "I don't blame you," I said, unsure whether I was lying or not.

"I don't believe you," he said bluntly. "You look at your hands when you feel bad or guilty about something."

I raised my head, and we met eyes. His gaze held a bit of anger, but I knew it was anger toward himself.

"I'm not lying, Cassius. I am grateful for everything you did. Without you and Terry, I might never have gotten Bella back." I knew that was true. "Oh shit, I didn't call Rory!"

I picked up the phone and immediately pressed Rory's number on speed dial. He picked up in one ring. In a rush, I explained everything that had happened. The relief in his voice was evident, and he even asked to speak with Cassius. I handed over the phone and left the room to get a can of soda. When I came back, Cassius looked happier. I handed over a second can I'd bought for him, and he thanked me.

"May I hug you?" he asked after opening his can of cola and drinking deep.

I wasn't sure I was ready for that yet. Something made me hesitate. Then, before I knew it, he took rapid steps toward me and picked me up, holding me tight.

"Now is not the time to be pulling back, Natalia," he said as I stood robotically in his arms. "Our daughter needs the two of us. And I intend to make sure she gets all that she needs from us. And the thing I think she needs to know first is that I am her father."

"Give it a day," I said, relaxing slightly in his arms.

"No," he said firmly, "she has gone through her life thinking she doesn't have a father. She deserves to know. And I think it will be something to help her recover faster. Don't you agree?"

Did I? "I don't know, Cassius," I said, pulling away from him.

"Natalia," he said with an edge to his tone. "I am telling her that I am her father immediately once she wakes up."

I nodded and tried not to look down at my hands. "If you think it is for the best. But if she changes again, I will be upset."

"I think you should prepare for her to be changed from this experience. It would be a lot for anyone to handle, let alone a child. But they say children are resilient. Plus, as you can see, Bella likes me. I think it will make her happy."

He had scored a point there. Bella did seem to blossom when he was around.

"Fine," I said. "You should tell her. Just wait until we are at home and you are cuddling with her."

"I'll wait until then. I don't want to tell Bella that in the hospital. Thank you for letting me do this. It means a lot," he said, pulling me close.

He kissed where my neck and shoulder met. Goose bumps speckled my arms and chest.

It wasn't long before the doctor cleared for us to take her home. We had to wake her every two hours due to the mild concussion, but the worst of it would be dealing with her cast. I made sure it was pink so Bella would at least like the color.

Cassius carried her to the SUV, and we climbed in. We still had a security detail on us, just in case Tina had hired others. But I had a suspicion that her only help had been murdered in that old warehouse. I was still thankful for the extra security.

Bella woke up a bit as Cassius strapped her into the booster seat. "Cass-us, are we going home?"

"Yes, Bella, we are. Now get some sleep." He climbed in beside her and rubbed her head as she leaned on him.

Soon, she was sleeping again.

When we got home, Bella was awake enough to walk, holding my hand. We went inside, and I could see that Cassius wanted to break the news to Bella right away, so I decided to take the lead.

"Bella," I said softly. "We have something important to tell you."

She looked at me quizzically with her pale-blue eyes that matched her father's.

I continued, "You know how that kid at the day care made fun of you for not having a daddy?"

Bella looked down at her feet and nodded.

"Well, you do have a daddy."

She looked up at me with big eyes.

"Cassius is your daddy."

I didn't think Bella's eyes could get any bigger. She looked from me to Cassius and back to me again. "Cassius is my daddy?" I could sense her disbelief.

"Yes, Bella," Cassius intoned. "I am your dad."

Bella broke into a smile and ran to him, hugging his leg. "I knew it" was all she said. She raised her arms to be picked up, which Cassius did. They hugged for a long time, and I watched the touching scene silently.

"Mama?" Bella asked. "Can my daddy tuck me in? I'm tired. And what is this on my arm? It hurts."

Cassius began explaining to her about her arm, and she looked like she was about to cry for a minute but then seemed determined not to let herself shed a tear. Maybe she was more like me than I thought. I watched as she and Cassius went upstairs to her room, and I gave them their privacy.

I pulled the blanket off the back of the couch, curled up, and fell asleep instantly.

I woke the next day to discover that Cassius had left and that Bella was happily playing with her new teddy bear. He left me a note, and I picked it up and read it.

Natalia,

I am sorry for not waking you, but I knew you needed your sleep. I will be back later to pick you up for a date. Rory has agreed to watch Bella for us. I need to spend time with you. Aside from Bella, you are all I think about. I booked us a surprise date. Don't dress up. Wear something formfitting yet comfortable.

Cassius

I couldn't help but smile.

And then I started wondering what I had that was formfitting and comfortable. I had a pink tracksuit and decided that was what I would wear. Something in my gut told me to expect something out of the ordinary. But then I thought a tracksuit would not be acceptable attire, so I went to my closet and pulled out black leggings and knee-high boots. A pristine black long coat and a shimmery black long-sleeved shirt followed.

I couldn't choose between the two outfits, so I left them on the bed. I would decide in the moment.

I spent the morning playing with and doting on Bella. We made a pancake breakfast, went to my loft studio, and played with the clay. She was creating a castle. Despite the cast impeding her movements, I was happy to see her active and alert.

She had endured being woken up at all hours of the night by Cassius with little fuss. The sound of his alarm had woken me during my sleep once or twice. That I hadn't heard it every time spoke of how exhausted I had been.

At lunch, Cassius showed up on a motorcycle. I had no idea what he was thinking—*me on a bike?*

"I know what you're thinking. Get changed. We have an adrenalizing day ahead of us."

"Adrenalizing?" I felt a bit panicky. "Don't you think we have all been adrenalized enough over the past few days?"

"Nah." He gave me a cocky grin. "You can handle it."

I liked the vote of confidence. Hearing it from Cassius's mouth delighted me.

I went upstairs and put on my black outfit. When I tried it on, it was perfect. I looked almost like a biker chick. I did a quick swipe of eyeliner on my lower lids and put on some mascara and a matte nude lipstick I'd fallen in love with. As I walked down the stairs, Cassius whistled.

"It's not too... black?" I asked uncertainly.

"No, you look perfect."

The heated look he gave me seared my soul. His gaze instantly aroused me, and I averted my eyes and strolled down the stairs. Bella ran up and gave me a hug. Rory came out with a box of crackers and a cheese-and-meat plate. We all had some together, seated in the living room.

A little voice piped up. "What does a daddy do?"

"What do you mean?" I asked.

"I don't know," Bella said quickly and stuck a finger in her mouth. I would have to break her of that habit if I could. It was a giveaway that she was uncomfortable.

"Well," Cassius started, "we give airplane rides and cuddle. We hold teddy bear picnics and race cars. And we make excellent cheesecakes."

Bella giggled and wrapped her arms around his neck. Her cast was awkward, and she asked for an airplane ride, but he said no because of her arm. Instead, he promised her a teddy bear picnic later, then we left.

I hung on for dear life during the motorcycle ride. We headed toward the countryside and pulled into the yard of a massive redbrick house.

"Who lives here?" I asked, curious.

"We do," he said.

"W-What?" I sputtered.

"I'm kidding. This house belongs to the guy who's side-by-side we are buying. Ever driven a side-by-side before?" he asked.

I shook my head.

"Well, get ready for a fun time because we are buying one today and taking it for a trip."

He went inside and came out with the keys, waving for me to follow. We circled the house to find a black-and-white ATV.

"We're taking it for a spin today. I'll come and pick it up with a trailer tomorrow. There are a lot of nice trails around here. We'll do some exploring."

I got in the vehicle, feeling a bit tense. It had been years since I'd been on a four-wheeler, snowmobile, or any other recreational vehicle. Cassius fastened me in and plopped a helmet on my head.

"You want to drive?" he asked.

"Maybe later," I said, and by later, I meant never.

He revved the engine, and we took off at a speed I was very uncomfortable with. When he turned, I thought for sure we were going to tip over, but then I realized he was very familiar with how these things worked.

Soon, despite my trepidation, I was actually enjoying the experience. We hit bumps and went flying over others. My heart raced, and I hung on for dear life, but soon I was breathing heavily and smiling wildly. After a while, I was no longer scared and was having the time of my life. Every once in a while, Cassius would look over at me, giving me his crooked grin.

Soon he tapped the fuel gauge. "Time to head back. Do you want to drive?"

I eagerly said yes, and we switched spots. Feeling the power of the machine made my adrenaline rise, and we were soon driving rather slowly back to the house. I was still thrilled, though. When we pulled up, Cassius leaned over and unbuckled the chin strap of my helmet, carefully pulling it off my head. He kissed me then, and I wanted to crawl into his lap. I was so turned on.

"Take me to your home," I whispered.

"Yes, ma'am," he said, scooping me up and carrying me to the bike. With me clinging to his back like a monkey, we quickly made it to his house in the suburbs.

We pulled right into his garage, and I began fondling him. Kissing the side of his face and neck, I unbuckled his pants and released his hard cock. I leaned down and began sucking it, kneeling on the concrete floor.

"Oh, Natalia," he moaned, "you're killing me."

I gave him a coy smile and again took his thick cock into my mouth. I sucked hard and fast, and soon I was tasting his precum. I lifted my head, massaging his dick with my hand.

Suddenly, he picked me up and threw me over his shoulder like a sack of potatoes. He strolled inside and plopped me down on the first couch he saw. He slid my leggings down and began licking my clitoris. I was already wet, turned on from sucking his cock, but he devoured me. He pressed me hard into the couch by my hips, and as his tongue flicked, I began shuddering with plea-sure. Small moans escaped my mouth, and soon, I was holding the back of his head hard against my pussy and grinding myself on his face.

His fingers slid up my body and under my shirt. He lifted my bra and began massaging my nipples with his fingertips. When I came, I cried out and felt my juices soak his chin. He flipped me over then and raised me by my hips, licking me again but this time also probing my hole with his fingers. He rammed them into my G-spot, and soon I was coming again. No man had ever paid as much attention to my pleasure as Cassius did.

He pulled away, and I heard his pants falling to the floor. I was ready for him to enter me, and he did so very slowly, letting me feel how he filled me up. But I didn't want slow sex. I wanted him to pound me like a jackhammer.

"Fuck me hard, Cassius," I begged him.

He began picking up speed with his thrusts.

Soon my face was pressed hard into the couch, and I was crying out with each rapid thrust of his hips. The slapping noises as our flesh smacked together made me squirt all over his cock. I felt my fluids leaking onto what must have been an expensive couch.

"Ride me, my love," he ordered me.

I pulled the leggings off completely but kept the boots on for fun. I stood before him and rubbed my clit, giving him a little show. His eyes were glazed with lust. He reached forward, grabbed me, and pulled me on top as I straddled him. I plopped down on his cock, and he moaned. And I don't know what took over, but I grabbed him by the hair and pulled his head back so his throat was bared to me. I began sucking on his neck, and my hips moved rhythmically.

We fucked like that for a while before he grabbed firmly onto my hips and began controlling the motion. He pulled my pussy hard against his dick over and over. I spasmed and started crying out in pain laced with sweetness. I squirted again, but I felt his cock throb and empty inside me this time. He grunted, his breathing hard. I didn't get up and instead collapsed in his arms, panting heavily. We stayed like that for a while as our fluids leaked all over the couch.

"I hope this thing wasn't too expensive," I said, a faint blush rising to my cheeks.

"I would let this whole house burn if it meant making love to you like that again."

I threw my head back and laughed. When Bella had gone missing, I had never thought I would love and laugh again. But here I was, with a man I adored, who was quickly capturing my heart.

A few days later, after numerous lovemaking sessions and dates, ten teddy bear picnics, and days and nights spent together as a family, we went to see Bella's psychologist, Mrs. VanAllen. She spent some time with Bella, then let Cassius and me into the room to speak with her.

"It's a pleasure to meet you, Mr. Baxter," she said as we entered her office. "I have good news for the two of you."

"What?" I couldn't help but ask.

"There is a profound difference in Bella. She was more active and engaged than ever. Despite what she went through, she seems to have bounced back at an amazing rate. I think the relationship she has formed with her father has played a big role in her recovery, and I don't think she needs to see me for treatment any longer."

My mouth dropped open, and I exchanged a relieved look with Cassius. I grabbed him by the collar and laid a kiss on his pliant lips.

He flushed red before saying, "Thank you, Mrs. VanAllen. We couldn't have received better news."

A few weeks later, I was sitting in my office at work, looking over a brief, when a knock at the door jarred me out of my concentration. "Come in," I called.

Trinda opened the door with a big smile on her face. "I have a package for you to be opened immediately."

I sighed, wondering what had gone wrong. She passed me the legal-size manila envelope, and I slit it open with my letter opener, then pulled out the document and began reading.

Soon my eyes were as big as saucers. "Is this what I think it is?" I asked Trinda.

She shrugged and left the office, closing the door behind her. I couldn't believe what I was reading. I had been promoted to vice president of the board of directors. Only Cassius would be above me. I had wanted this for so long—to finally be recognized for my work and to further my career.

I scanned through the documents and signed them right then and there. At the end of the paper was an invitation to a party being held that afternoon. I broke into a grin. I rushed to Cassius's office and was surprised to see he wasn't there. I asked Vera where he was, but she just shrugged. When I turned around, everyone in the office was on their feet.

"Congrats, Nat!" someone yelled, then people were putting on party hats and wolf-whistling or clapping. Two tables were wheeled out of the staff room, one full of goodies and the other filled with a range of drinks. Then someone pushed out a massive box wrapped with a big bow.

"Open the present!" Vera yelled over the din.

I walked up to it wearing a grin. When I grabbed the bow and pulled, the box began opening itself. The workers around me threw ribbons in the air.

Out of the box rose Cassius. He wore a black tuxedo and carried sterling roses in one hand and a velvet ring box in the other. I covered my mouth with my hands, and tears began running down my cheeks.

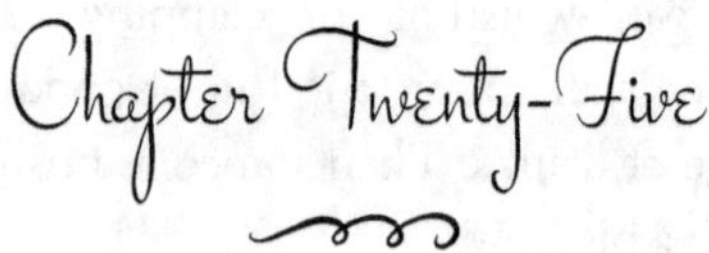

CASSIUS

When I popped out of that box and laid eyes on Natalia, I knew I hadn't made a mistake. She had covered her mouth, and tears poured out of her eyes. She began sniffling and wiping her tears away.

"Cassius?" she asked, as if she was confused. "What's happening?"

"Well," I started, "not only have you been promoted, but I am asking for your hand in marriage."

I pushed open the front of the box, walked toward her, and dropped down on one knee. "Natalia Blake." I swallowed hard, chasing away the knot in my throat. "You have changed my world for the better. I never realized how miserable I was until I got to know you and your loving ways. And now that we have a family, I want to do right by you. We deserve happiness, and I know nothing in this world would make me happier than spending the rest of my life with you. I never knew what a lonely existence I was living until you brought your light into my life. Even when you were challenging me every step of the way, I couldn't help but be intrigued and mystified."

I paused. "And since we got Bella back, I have never cherished anything like I do the two of you. I never want us to part, and I swear I will never stray or stop giving you all the love and attention you deserve. Your strength makes me want to be a better man, and your soul entraps mine."

I opened the ring box. It was the largest diamond I could find, and it was flawless. I held it up for her to see. "Natalia, will you do me the honor of marrying me?"

She was sobbing and hiccupping. Every employee was silent, waiting for her answer. She crumpled down onto her knees, and I grabbed her, afraid she was fainting. Instead, she wrapped her arms around me and gave me a salty kiss.

"Of course, I'll marry you, Cassius Baxter. I love you and always will."

I grabbed the ring out of the box, and she held up her hand. I slipped the ring on and kissed her fingertips. I lifted her back to her feet and wrapped my arms around her, losing myself in her kiss.

All the employees roared their approval, and soon, there was music playing, and everyone was toasting Natalia and me.

The festivities lasted well past supper, and then it was just Natalia and me left. I picked her up, and she wrapped her legs around my hips. I kissed her softly on the lips.

"I want to make love to you in my office," I said, hoping she wouldn't deny me.

She answered me by pulling my head to her and kissing me hungrily. She tasted of champagne and vanilla cupcakes. With every step closer to my office, my cock got harder. We kissed madly with such heat that I felt like I was burning up with a fever.

I carried her into my office and set her down. I swept what was on my desk to the floor, picking her up and laying her on the mahogany top. I lifted her pencil skirt over her ample hips and tore her shirt open. I kissed down her neck and chest, then I pulled my pants down. When my engorged cock was in the open air, I felt it throb in anticipation.

I pulled her legs over my shoulders and kissed her pubic bone and inner thighs, taunting her by giving her clit a lick. I explored her groin with my tongue and lips until she was squirming.

"Oh my God, Cassius. Please lick it. You're torturing me."

"That's kind of the point," I said with a cocky tone, but I did as Natalia asked.

She was sopping wet, and my tongue made circles around the tip of her clit. I slipped one, then two, fingers inside and began finger fucking her fast and hard. Soon she was gyrating and screaming out my name. Her juices coated my fingers, and I stuck them in her mouth, making her taste herself.

She grabbed my hand and sucked each one of my fingers seductively. I wanted to be inside her so badly, but I flipped her over and pushed up the back of her shirt and dress coat. I kissed her lower back and nibbled my way to her firm ass before spreading her cheeks with my hands and licking her anus. I had never done that to a woman, and I found that it was very arousing.

I looked up to see her gazing at me over her shoulder. She looked punch-drunk, and I couldn't help but slide a finger in her ass. She tensed up at first but then loosened her sphincter.

Grabbing my cock in my hand, I rubbed it up and down her moist slit. When the tip was near her anus, I thrust slightly, and the head of my cock slid into her asshole. She moaned and reached her arms back, spreading her cheeks wider for me.

"You want to fuck my tight little hole?" she asked huskily.

"You have no idea how much I want to fuck both your holes," I said honestly.

"Spit on it and slide it in. I want you to. I've never done it before, but I am willing to try. I'd do anything for you, Cassius."

I leaned down and licked her ass again. This time, I spat on it, then on the head of my cock. I stroked it so the spit lubed it up. Then I set the tip of my cock to her puckered hole. "Do you want me to go slow or fast?" I asked. I wanted her to be comfortable.

"I don't know," she said, her voice quivering. "Whatever you think is best."

"I'll surprise you then."

I guided my cock slowly inside her asshole. Once the tip was in, my hips jerked, and I filled her ass with my cock. She began moaning loudly. I went at a slow pace, and I felt her tremble.

"Are you okay?" I asked, still pumping away at her ass in long, slow strokes.

"Yes, play with my clit. I want to cum again."

I reached my hand down and rubbed her slippery, wet clit hard. I picked up the pace of my hips and fingers, and soon she was pushing back on me. I felt her asshole tighten, then spasm as she cried out. Fluid dripped down my fingers, and the sensation made me almost blow my load.

I pulled out slowly and wiped my cock with my kerchief. Then, I flipped Natalia over and laid my body on top of hers. I kissed her, slid my cock inside her vagina, and rocked my hips leisurely. She grabbed my ass and pulled me hard inside of her, biting my shoulder and lifting her hips to meet mine. I bit her back, and she made groans of pleasure.

The wet noises and the throaty sounds she was making thrilled me. I pumped her hard, jarring the desk. She tightened her pussy around my thick dick, and I moaned at how tight she was. Soon, I was coming inside her.

"Oh, Natalia," I cried as my dick spurted inside her wet hole. Even after the last drop emptied into her, I still couldn't stop fucking her. "You have no idea what you do for me. I love you," I said, collapsing on top of her.

"I love you, too, Cassius."

We just held each other for a long moment. I then stood up, and she got to her feet. She looked well and thoroughly fucked. Her hair was in disarray, and her shirt was ripped beyond repair.

"Did I hurt you?" I asked, concerned. I knew I had a large cock and was worried I may have hurt her when I fucked her ass.

She shook her head. "It felt so taboo. But I am happy I got to try it with you. I kind of liked it," she replied, blushing deeply. She stood up and pulled her panties back on before smoothing the skirt over her hips. She looked down at her shirt and buttoned up her dress jacket.

I pulled my pants up and looked at all the cum that coated the desk and dripped onto the floor. "I should probably clean that up," I said.

"No," Natalia said, then she slid the skirt back up and laid on the desk again. "I want you to lick me clean and make me cum through my panties. You tried your taboo dream. Now it's my turn." The look she gave me was almost devilish.

I positioned myself between her legs and began lapping gently at her panties. They were soaked with our fluids. I slid my tongue under the satiny fabric, rubbing the head of her clit with the back of my tongue. She wriggled, and I pinned her hips down. Her fingers entwined in my hair as I took long, slow licks. Soon, her chest was heaving, and I picked up the pace. I realized I was getting hard again. *Who knew something like this would turn me on so much?*

"Cassius!" she screamed, then she was shuddering.

I held her hips firmly as a fresh wave of fluid coated my chin. But I didn't stop licking. In fact, I pressed my tongue and chin into her harder. "Cum for me again, baby," I said and sucked hard on her clit. I jammed my fingers inside her.

"Oh my God," she cried, "I can't take it!"

"Yes," I said from between her shapely legs. "You can and you will." And I bit and flicked her clit.

She was sobbing and twitching by the time I finished her off again. Sweat was pouring from her face and her perky, pink-tipped breasts.

Natalia sat up and pulled me in for a kiss. "That was the best lovemaking I have ever had," she said before collapsing back on the desk, giggling. I couldn't help but laugh with her.

"It's not over yet," I said, undoing my pants to reveal my hard dick.

She fell on her knees and took my throbbing cock between her lips. It wasn't long before I emptied myself into her hungry mouth, calling out her name, then I fell to the floor beside her.

Epilogue

NATALIA

"I do," Cassius said triumphantly.

"You may now kiss the bride," said the priest.

Cassius bent down and gave me a chaste kiss. The wedding guests cheered, and music started playing as we made our way down the aisle as newlyweds. Cassius stopped near my parents and shook hands with them before picking up Bella and following me out of the church.

There was a short reception before Cassius and I headed out on his private jet for a honeymoon in Trinidad and Tobago.

"Why can't I come, daddy?" Bella asked for the hundredth time.

"Because this trip is just for your mother and me. We will have a longer vacation with you once we get back. I promise."

Bella stuck out her tongue, then sulked.

"Bella," I warned, "if you act up, then there won't be another vacation for you to go on. And you haven't seen your grandparents in ages. You will have fun with them at their place. And once our honeymoon is over, we will come and get you."

"Okay, Mama," she said, dispirited.

Since her kidnapping, Bella had grown more confident and

was quickly on her way to becoming a stubborn, smart-ass like her father. He said she was taking after me, but we both knew she mimicked him the most.

As we exited, the wedding guests who managed to get out ahead of us rained rice down upon us. And I was shocked to see not a limousine but a 1967 Chevy Impala sitting at the bottom of the stairs. I looked at Cassius, and he grinned crookedly.

"It's your wedding present," he said. "I know you always wanted one, thanks to Rory. Speaking of which."

He gestured, and Rory walked up and set the car keys in my hand, then he held his hands out to take Bella.

"And there is another surprise. We're not going to the reception. We are going to make your dreams come true."

I was totally bewildered. *My dreams?*

"Say goodbye to Bella." He passed her over to me, and I hugged her.

"I'm not sure what's going on, but we'll see you in a week, baby girl." I kissed her, and she hugged me tightly.

"Bye, Mama."

Then Rory led her away.

"Get in the car. We're going for a drive."

I unhooked my puffy skirts and revealed the slinkier dress underneath. Cassius looked at me with wide eyes.

"You can't expect me to drive in that dress."

He shrugged and climbed into the passenger side.

I slid behind the wheel of my new car and shivered in delight. I turned it on and listened to the purr of the engine. "Where to?" I asked.

"111 Swift Road," he said.

"Okay?" As far as I knew, there were only offices on that street.

As we were driving there, he began to talk. "Do you remember how you told me you wanted to start your own business?"

"Yes, and I remember you dissuading me every chance you got," I said matter-of-factly.

"Well," he said, "I've had a change of heart."

"What do you mean?" I asked, pulling onto the street. And then I saw what he meant. Across the front of the building was a big red bow.

"That's your new office building. I've had it gutted, and it is ready for you to choose the interior design once we get back from our honeymoon. And here." He handed me an envelope.

I ripped it open and saw a check. It was for ten million dollars.

"This is a bit of start-up money. You always wanted to start your own business, and now you can."

I was speechless. "But I don't even know what type of business I want to own!" I exclaimed.

"Well, now you have to figure that out for yourself."

I made to get out of the car, but he grabbed my arm. "You can look at it in due time. There is one more stop before we leave for the airport. Go to 654 Dixon Road."

"I have no idea where that is." I was still in shock.

"I'll guide you," Cassius said.

After following his directions, I pulled into the entry of a walled-in property with a security gate and a guard. I made to stop at the booth, but the guard opened the doors and waved us in. There was a long driveway, and I saw horses running in a field.

"Where are we?" I asked.

All he did was grin. "Keep driving," he said.

And then I saw a beautiful manor. There were elaborate gardens and a garage that would fit at least ten cars. When I pulled up in front of the building, I saw four-wheelers, the side-by-side he'd bought, and then I knew what this place was. It was our new home.

"Did you buy this place too?"

He nodded, smiling with his dazzling-white teeth. "Wait until you see the master suite. And Bella has a whole wing to herself. We also have ten horses, three pools, and a sauna, a gym for us that is fully outfitted, and a dance studio for Bella. Our bathroom has a glass-walled shower and a hot tub. Not to mention, I have hired staff to keep the property well taken care of."

"Cassius, you didn't have to buy us this."

"I know. I wanted you two to have the luxury I grew up with but be loving parents to our daughter, unlike my parents."

His face darkened for a second, and I reached over and laid a hand on his thigh.

"Oh," he said, "and we won't need to go to the airport. We have our own airstrip, and I bought you a small plane."

"What?"

He handed me a ring of keys. "I asked Rory what you have always wanted to do, and he told me you wanted to learn how to fly. So I have arranged for flying lessons. We can even skydive if you want. I got all the gear for that too."

"Oh, Cassius." Tears were coming. I did not want to ruin my makeup, so I stopped before too much damage occurred. "And here I thought I got you the perfect gift. I bought you a Rolex and that street bike you wanted."

"I already got my gift," he said, lifting my hand and kissing my fingers. "I received your hand in marriage. That's the best gift I could wish for."

"I have another gift for you too."

He looked at me quizzically.

"I'm pregnant." This time, I couldn't stop the tears.

With fiery passion, we embraced and kissed each other thoroughly.

Cassius carried me across the threshold of our new home, and we made love right in the foyer.

It was the best day of my life.

www.ingramcontent.com/pod-product-compliance
Lightning Source LLC
Chambersburg PA
CBHW071941150726
47999CB00001B/282